Other Nick Polo books by Jerry Kennealy

Polo in the Rough
Polo's Ponies
Polo Solo
Polo, Anyone?

Polo's Wild Card

POLO'S
WILD
CARD

Jerry Kennealy

ST. MARTIN'S PRESS
NEW YORK

Design by Amelia R. Mayone

Library of Congress Cataloging-in-Publication Data

Kennealy, Jerry.
    Polo's wild card.
        p.   cm.
    "A Thomas Dunne book."
    ISBN 0-312-04437-2
I. Title.
    PS3561.E4246P65 1990   813'.54—dc20   89-77954

10   9   8   7   6   5   4   3   2

*This book is
dedicated to my mother,
with fond memories
from a very lucky son*

Polo's Wild Card

"Five hundred dollars," said Jane Tobin, smiling. A piece of raisin from her Waldorf salad was stuck between her two upper front teeth.

"Five hundred dollars," I repeated loudly enough to cause the middle-aged couple sitting at the table next to us to snap their necks around. They were both wearing light-colored cotton outfits, dressed for summer: summer in Los Angeles or Palm Springs, but not summer in San Francisco. Before they got back to their hotel their teeth would be chattering.

Jane gave me a shushing sound. "It's for a very good charity."

They both gave Jane an appraising look: the woman's one of disgust, the man's calculating the price versus the goods. His eyes wandered leisurely over Jane, taking in her auburn hair, creamy complexion, and the way her blouse bulged nicely. He seemed disappointed that the table concealed her legs.

We were having dinner in Bix's, one of the hotter spots on the current San Francisco restaurant scene. It was done in art deco, with a fifty-foot ceiling. There was a long mahogany bar and a grand piano, where a tall, blond torch singer was doing justice to "Love Me or Leave Me." Jane had read a review that said Bix's "was the kind of spot Nick and Nora Charles would pick for cocktails before a night on the town." Who could ask for a better review than that?

"You've got something between your teeth," I told Jane. "And I know it's a very good charity. But if you made an alphabetical list of all the worthy charities that deserved that kind of a donation, I'd break my bank account before you got to the letter *B*."

"It's deductible," she said, then went fishing for the raisin bit with the tip of her napkin. Jane was a three-times-a-week columnist for the *San Francisco Bulletin* and enjoyed a nice, guaranteed weekly paycheck, as well as a small, but handy, expense account. Her paper was unknowingly buying us dinner.

"The trouble with you salaried employees," I said, "is that you think anyone who is in business for themselves can go out and spend money on anything they want, as long as it's deductible. The problem is, you've got to make the money before you can deduct it, and even then good old Uncle Sam only lets you write off a small amount."

"Poor baby," Jane said, digging back into her salad. "I just thought you'd like to go to this affair with me."

"I love affairs with you, darling, but the price is a little stiff on this one. Can't your paper cover two tickets?"

"You're lucky they're popping for dinner." A young waiter came over and took the wine bottle from its cooler and topped off our glasses. I noticed that the couple sitting next to us had edged their chairs our way.

"Look," Jane said. "I know it's expensive, but there will be excellent food and wine. I've bought a new dress." She actually stooped to batting the long lashes over her green eyes at me. "It's blue velvet, low cut, and has those thin little spaghetti straps that you love so much."

I toasted her with my glass. "Sounds wonderful, Jane, but—"

2

"And I've been assured there will be a high-stakes poker game going on all night."

I stopped the wineglass before it reached my mouth. "Poker? Who told you that?"

"Harry Jupiter. He's mad because the *Examiner* won't sponsor him."

Jupiter was the ace sports reporter for the city's afternoon newspaper, and a devoted poker player. One of the minor problems of living in San Francisco is that it's really a small town, and if you have a reputation of being very good, or very bad, at something, word soon gets around, and people start avoiding you. Harry and I have been known to drive to Los Angeles just to get into a card game with strangers.

"A poker game. And you think I could sit in on this game?"

"All it takes is a ticket to the party and a tuxedo, Nick."

"Hmmmmm. How much did you say this was going to cost me?"

She smiled triumphantly. "Five hundred dollars."

I turned my head so I was sure my voice would carry to our noisy neighbors. "Is that for all night?"

The woman bounced her frosty eyes between Jane and me. The man smiled and nodded his head approvingly.

2

The House the Homeless benefit was held in a private residence in Pacific Heights. It was on a corner, the outside brick and ivy, and of a size that could pass for a small hotel. Our cab turned into the driveway and let us out.

Music spilled out of the front door as Jane and I walked up the curving polished cement stairs. A young man, who at least had the guts not to look embarrassed while wearing long white stockings and a plum-colored silk outfit with a ruffled white shirt and powdered wig, stood in front of the opened door. He looked like one of the guys who brought King Henry VIII his wine in a *Masterpiece Theatre* production.

He accepted our invitations with a "Thank you kindly" that sounded more like the Mission District than tony London.

A similarly dressed guy came over and asked for Jane's coat. She hadn't been lying about her dress: soft blue velvet that plunged low enough to reveal what she now called her "treasure chest." Jane had not been born so endowed, and after she'd divorced her first husband, commonly called "the bastard," her mother had insisted on treating Jane to "the best boob job money can buy." "Let the bastard drool" was one of Mom's favorite sayings, according to Jane.

4

I once asked her why a bright, attractive, intelligent woman would bother with that particular form of cosmetic surgery. At the time of the question I was admiring the results, and probably drooling a little bit myself. Her explanation: "Dave [the bastard] always stared at busty young things, saying, 'If you've got it, flaunt it.' Well, now I've got it, and I'm enjoying flaunting it."

She flaunted her way farther into the room. The crowd was mostly in their fifties, with a smattering of pretty young things flaunting things the way Jane was. The ladies' dresses were mostly black or white, mostly silk and long, mostly off one or both shoulders. The men were in tuxedos of a variety of colors: dark blue, light blue, white; one lavender tails outfit that would have made Fred Astaire blush.

I was in a rental basic black job: plain white shirt, black ready-tied tie, and black cummerbund. I hate wearing tuxedos. I'm always afraid people will think I'm either a singer or a waiter. So far no one had asked me for an hors d'oeuvre or to sing "Volare." I drew the line at the shoes the rental joint supplied: little patent-leather pumps with bows on them. Maryjanes, I think we called them as kids. My polished loafers hadn't caused any fingers to be pointed so far.

Jane was shaking hands and introducing me to flush-faced people who said, "Nice to meet you," without meaning it. Waiters, in tuxedos much better fitting than mine, wandered through the crowd carrying trays with small stemmed glasses of champagne. The glasses were of the same design that you find at "champagne brunches," where you're allowed all the wine you can drink, the glasses so shallow that you're getting it by the thimbleful. Figuring that the five-hundred-dollar entry fee entitled me to at least my full share, I started picking the glasses off the tray two at a time.

Someone at a grand piano that was dwarfed by the size of the room was pouring out show tunes. Buffet tables covered with thick snow-white linen lined one wall. The tables were filled with an assortment of polished silver food trays, some with the glow of butane flames under them.

5

"Having a good time?" Jane asked.

"You did mention something about a high-stakes poker game, didn't you?"

She patted my cheek patronizingly. "You wouldn't want them to start the game while everyone was still sober, would you?"

I shook hands with some more people, most of whom looked as if they were out of a William Hamilton "Now Society" cartoon. Ah, the idle rich. So easy to ridicule: overdressed, oversexed, overindulgent, yet, without their support, the opera, ballet, and most art galleries would go under, as would many of the needy charities their swank parties supported. At least they had a legitimate reason for being there: to have a good time and show off their latest clothes and jewelry. I was there for a card game.

Someone tapped me on the shoulder.

When I turned, a tall, broad-shouldered guy with blond hair and a sunburned forehead was there.

"Could I see you for a minute?" he asked, then pivoted around and walked away before I could answer. I watched his back retreat a few yards into the crowd; then he turned back and looked surprised when I wasn't there.

He stomped back with a stern expression on his face.

I watched him as he approached. It was a good six years since I had seen Roy Whitman. I wished it were more like a good twenty years. He made the papers every once in a while, stories about his working for some rich and famous person who was divorcing some other rich and famous person, and one of them had hired private investigator Roy Whitman. He worked the "stolen children" game, seeming to find the kids only in exotic places such as Hawaii, Japan, or the south of France. Doesn't mommy or daddy ever snatch the kids and take off to places like Turlock or Rapid City?

Whitman's ad in the yellow pages, which featured a picture of him taken years ago, listed him as an expert in "personal problems and protection."

He looked as if he had added a few inches to his waist-line and another under his chin since I last spoke to him. The bulge over his left hip wasn't fat, though; his white dinner jacket swung open as he walked, showing the handle of a large revolver.

"I thought we were going to talk," he said.

I looked into his beady eyes. "What's wrong with right here?"

He folded his arms across his chest. "I'm in charge of security," he said, as if it meant something.

"Good for you, Roy. Make sure you count the silver."

One of the omnipresent waiters came by, and I exchanged two empty glasses for full ones.

Jane walked over toward us, saw the expression on my face, and swiveled back to the people she'd been talking to.

Whitman moved in close and bent his head down. At six two, he had a couple of inches on me. "I'm in charge of security, Polo, and I worry when I see an ex-con mingling with the guests."

My, my. Such bitterness, and just because I spent a few months in a federal prison for stumbling over five hundred thousand in cash and not mentioning it to Uncle Sam. "That must ruin your social life, Roy boy. The only reason you didn't end up with striped pajamas is that you cried so much, you damn near floated out of the courtroom."

He closed his eyes, straightened to his fullest height, opened his eyes, then, in a harsh whisper, said, "How did you get in here, Polo?"

"I paid, Roy. The full five hundred dollars. Does that give me the right to complain about the security?"

He jabbed a long, pointy finger into my starched shirt. "Just remember, buddy boy, you did time, and I didn't."

He did an about-face a Marine sergeant would have been proud of and left me there alone with my two champagne glasses.

Jane came over and relieved me of one of the glasses. "Who was the hunk?"

I felt like telling her just what Whitman was a hunk of, but settled for, "Just another private investigator."

"I found out where the poker game is, Nick."

"Bingo," I said, drinking from the one and only glass in my hand.

"No, poker. What do you think this is? A church bazaar?"

3

I followed Jane's bare, lightly freckled back down a long, narrow hallway. The walls were green, the shade of ripe Gravenstein apples. The ceiling was a pale blue. The walls were crammed with paintings, both oils and watercolors, charcoals, and some small, Egyptian sarcophagus masks protected by Lucite box-frames.

The hardwood floor was polished so brightly, you could almost see your reflection.

"You seem to know your way around here, Jane."

"I stopped by yesterday; Lionel gave me a tour."

"Lionel?"

She stopped and gave me an appraising look. "Lionel Martel. Haven't you heard of him, Nick?"

"Is he the guy they named the toy trains after? Lionel. What the hell did they call him in school? Li? Nel? Who is he?"

"Really, Nick. If they printed my column alongside the racehorse handicaps, maybe you'd read it more often. I did a whole article on Lionel. This is his family home. Lionel's father, Claude, is in Europe right now. When the auditorium backed out on holding the charity ball because of insurance problems, Lionel volunteered the house for tonight's party."

"And just what does Lionel do? Other than throw big parties when Daddy is away."

"He helps manage their holdings. They're very big in real estate, not only in the United States, but in Europe and the Far East. And they still have their art galleries, of course."

Of course. We came to a closed door. Jane tapped a ringed finger on it, then opened it without waiting for an answer. The room was mostly wood; polished oak from the look of it; bare wood flooring, paneled walls, studded with more paintings, a pool table, and against the far wall, a round table, the top covered with the same green felt as the pool table. Five men sat around the table. They gave us a cursory glance, then went back to their main concern, a card game.

Jane patted one of the seated men on his shoulder. "Lionel, this is my friend Nick. He was hoping to get into the game."

Lionel Martel looked up at Jane and smiled. He was a good-looking guy in his late thirties, with dark hair just going gray at the temples. His eyes were dark, with droopy lids that the ladies would think were sexy. He kept the smile on his face and turned to me and extended a hand. "Delighted, Nick. Any friend of Jane's is more than welcome. Grab a chair." He let go of my hand and put his on Jane's arm. "Care to try your luck, Jane? Or maybe you can just stay around and change mine."

I was introduced to the other players, on a first-name basis only: Chuck, Victor, Larry, and Bob. Victor, Bob, and Larry all wore well-tailored tuxedos. Chuck's was cut Western style, and his tie was one of those string things that the bankers and gamblers always wore in cowboy movies.

Jane stuck around the first three hands, which were not all that exciting. Since this was after all a charity event, I was informed that ten percent of each pot would be taken out and turned over to the House the Homeless committee.

They were playing dealer's choice, and we went from five-card stud, to seven-card stud, to jacks or better. On my deal I went to five-card and made a small profit. We were using chips, big, bright, shiny square ones; blues a hundred, reds fifty, and whites ten dollars.

After Jane left, it was Chuck's deal. There was the usual brief chatter between hands.

Chuck asked, "What kinda work you in, Nick?"

Tricky question under the circumstances. Victor looked prosperous enough to be just about anything, and from what I gathered from the chitchat, Larry and Bob were stockbrokers, and Chuck was in banking. If I told the truth, that I was a private investigator, not only would that put me on a much lower social scale than they were, but there would be those who would think that they were playing cards with either a sharpie or someone whom their wife hired to keep an eye on them. If you say you're a doctor, before long they'll ask some medical advice: a lawyer, legal advice. A stockbroker, what's hot in the market? So I gave the one-word answer that usually stops any repeat questions. "Insurance," I said. No one wants or needs any more insurance. Especially during a card game.

Chuck called out his choice of game, "Seven-card stud, low hole-card wild, roll your own, last card up."

There were groans around the table.

"Jesus, Chuck," Lionel said, "can't we just play real poker?"

"Dealer's choice, ain't it, partner?" Chuck said, smiling. "Got to get a little excitement in the game now and then, don't we, fellas?"

That kind of poker would never have been allowed in a legitimate, or for that matter, illegitimate game played by adults over the age of fifteen. It ranked right along with gimmick hands like baseball, or spit in the ocean. But since I was a new man in town, I didn't want to make waves. When in Rome, etc., etc.

11

Chuck dealt out three cards to everyone, each face-down. It's the kind of game where you can end up having four aces, and lose to someone with five of a kind. Chuck ended up winning the pot. He laughed as he raked in his winnings. "That's what I call a little excitement."

Lionel was in charge of selling the chips, and he and Bob reached into their wallets and bought a thousand dollars more.

Everyone has his own little way of checking out card players: The look in their eyes is the conventional wisdom. Or their habits, nervous tics, the way they hold the cards: if they look at their cards too much, not enough, that kind of thing. With me it's fingernails. Are they chewed at the ends? Filed down and lacquered? Cut short, long, dirty, neglected? They all told little secrets. Lionel's were cut down as far as they'd go, and there were little nicks that looked as if teeth had been nibbling there. His hands kept dancing around, from his cards to his chips to his lap.

Victor, Larry, and Bob all had nice, neatly trimmed jobs, with the cuticle showing. Regular businessmen's hands, which once in a while got a treatment while they sat in the barber's chair.

Chuck's were a little long, but filed down, and there was the shine of clear polish on them. The nails definitely didn't go with the rest of him. Even sitting down he was a big man, with an athlete's shoulders. He was past his fifties, and his face had more than its share of wrinkles, pits, moles, and blotches where a dermatologist had burned off spots of skin cancer. It was an outdoor face that went with his voice, a big, rough and tough cowpoke. His hands were big and calloused, but the fingernails looked as if they could have been working behind a blackjack table at Vegas. He was the one to look out for, so I set out a couple of traps.

If anyone at the table was studying my fingernails, they'd see some small dabs of the gray paint from my tenant's bathroom that hadn't gotten scraped away.

12

The game went on for over an hour, and I was comfortably ahead some three or four hundred dollars.

Bob had been the big loser and was smart enough to know it, so he left for the dance floor.

Jane came back for a minute, and there was a steady stream of waiters bringing in food and drink.

The chatter swayed from sports to politics, and I got the feeling that if anyone at the table identified themselves as a liberal, there could have been bloodshed.

Chuck called for another one of his goofy "roll your own" games again, and when I peeked at my three down cards, I saw a four of spades, the king of diamonds, and the four of diamonds. I rolled over the king, which, since my fours were low, for the moment gave me three kings.

The liquor had loosened up the betting, with Lionel gulping down more than his share. Chuck bumped the ante a hundred after turning over his card, a queen of hearts.

The problem with this type of poker game, and no doubt the reason Chuck usually picked it, is that everyone wants to stay in the pot until the end, because until the final, seventh card is dealt faceup, no one is sure just how good their hole cards are. Which means if you had a pair of say, sixes as the low, and therefore wild cards in your hand, and the last card you get is say a three, it throws away your whole strategy, because the three is now lower than your sixes. Confusing? Chuck was hoping you'd think that.

My final card couldn't have been better. The four of hearts, matching my two hole cards, meaning that now I had three fours, and they were the low cards, and thus wild cards, and by combining them with the other cards I'd been dealt—jack of clubs, king of clubs, and a rather useless six of clubs—I could make just about anything from five kings to a royal flush out of my hand. In this goofy game, with four wild cards, five of a kind was the high hand.

The betting got heavy, with Lionel staying with Chuck and me until the bitter end.

"I don't know what old Lionel is hiding there," Chuck said, "but you, Nick my boy, are bluffing your ass off. That last card knocked you off your horse, boy. I'm betting that you've got at best four kings." He pulled a small cigar out of his jacket pocket and lit it with a gold lighter. No kitchen matches against the thumbnail for this cowpoke. "You're a pretty good card player, Nick, but since it ain't likely we'll be playing together again, I'll tell you about a real bad habit you got, boy. Every time you're going to try and bluff, you put your chips on your hole cards." He patted his own hole cards. "Right there, son, you put your chips there. You've done it every hand you've run a bluff on. Just like you're doing now." He shook his head and threw three hundred-dollar chips into the pot. "It's an expensive lesson, boy, but one you'll thank me for later in life." He took a puff on his cigar and laughed as he blew out the smoke.

I let out a silent sigh of relief. I hadn't been sure that old Chuck had picked up on my little trap with the chips on the hole cards. I was home-free now.

Lionel groaned and threw in three hundred-dollar chips. "I've stayed this long, I might as well see just what you've got there, Chuck."

I dropped my chips into the pot. "Like the man said, as long as I've stayed this long."

Bodine had the five of diamonds, ten of diamonds, queen of spades, and queen of diamonds showing. He flipped over one hole card, the eight of hearts. No help there. Then he smiled and turned over the last two hole cards, the five of spades and queen of hearts, giving him two fives for wild cards to combine with the three queens.

"Five queens," Chuck said, reaching out for the chips. "Five beautiful ladies." He stopped and smiled at Lionel and me. "Neither of you boys can top that, now can you?"

"Full house, damn it," Lionel said, throwing his cards onto the table.

Chuck just smiled wider and reached out his long arms. "Sorry about that, Nicky boy."

"Me, too, Chucky," I said, turning over my two fours. "I hate to sound like a male chauvinist, but I think my five kings knock your five beautiful ladies out of the game."

Chuck's arms froze over the chips. He kept them over the chips for a long time, like a man caught walking in his sleep. His eyes narrowed as he drew them back. "Guess I miscalculated with you, Nick."

"Easy to do. How about we try some plain old stud on this hand?" I said. It was then that the waiter with the dirty fingernails came and passed out a round of drinks.

4

I mean they were really dirty. Long, uneven, yellow jobs with enough earth under them to pot a fuchsia. He offered the drink tray around the table and I made eye contact with him. He looked right through me. His waiter's tuxedo made mine look as if it had come from Saville Row. It was too tight across the shoulders, and he looked as if he'd have trouble buttoning it over his paunch. His starched white shirt had carved deep, red trenches in his neck. He was somewhere in his midthirties, with short reddish hair that had leaked some dandruff down onto his tuxedo jacket. He had a surly look on his face, which was the only thing that made him look like a real waiter. As he handed me my glass of champagne, his coat sleeve pulled up and I noticed the outline of a tattoo. It looked like the bottom tip of a dagger.

After passing out the drinks, the waiter whispered something into Lionel Martel's ear.

Martel stood up, almost knocking the table over, and excused himself. "Sorry, gentlemen, a phone call."

We played two more hands before we all agreed enough was enough. Chuck smiled when he settled up with me.

"Nice playing with you, partner," he said. The smile grew a little frosty when he added, "I hope we meet up again real soon."

16

I ended up winners by some three thousand four hundred dollars, eight hundred of which was owed me by my party host, Mr. Lionel Martel.

I wandered back to the main ballroom. Jane was whirling in the arms of a tall, debonair-looking man with a smile on his lips and a gleam in his eye. In that blue dress, she could put a gleam in a statue's eye.

I nodded my way around, picking shrimp the size of crescent rolls off the food table, exchanging empty champagne glasses for full ones, and keeping an eye out for Lionel Martel.

The music went upbeat, and Jane and I tripped the light fantastic; at least she tripped the light, I almost tripped the couples who were unwise enough to get within loafer's distance of me.

There was more wine, more shrimp, more music, more dancing, but still no sign of Martel. The music slowed down, and during a rendition of "As Time Goes By," Jane started nibbling on my ear. It was time to leave. Martel and his poker losses could wait for another day.

I was getting Jane's coat when Roy Whitman came hurrying by. He put a hand on my shoulder.

"Don't try leaving now, buddy, just don't try it," he said, puffing in deep drafts of air.

"What's your problem, Whitman?" I said, shaking off his hand.

"The cops are on their way, and you ain't leaving until they get here."

I hoped that Martel or Chuck weren't such sore losers that they had signaled for the gendarmes.

Jane joined us.

"What's the problem, Nick?" she said.

"Are you with this guy, ma'am?" Whitman piped in.

"I certainly am," she said, squaring her shoulders as if she'd been insulted.

Whitman backed off a bit. "We've had a problem.

There's been a robbery, and I'd appreciate it if you didn't leave until the police arrive."

Problem. Robbery. Police. Jane's lovely face sobered up immediately. It lost all semblance of love and romance, that little glow of just the right amount of wine and music. It was replaced by that hard, no-nonsense, I'm-a-reporter-and-what-the-hell-is-going-on-here look.

In fact she said, "I'm a reporter, and what the hell is going on here?"

Whitman's eyes pivoted back and forth between us, then settled on me.

"She really a reporter?"

"Absolutely, one of the best," I said proudly, implying that being a reporter was an honorable profession.

Whitman's response summed up the feelings of quite a few people on just how honorable indeed that calling is. "Shit," he said.

We were saved from further descriptive renderings by the arrival of the police and an ambulance crew with a gurney. The paramedics wheeled the gurney toward the back of the house. I didn't know the first two uniformed cops, but when the plainclothes inspector walked in, it was my turn.

"Shit," I said, "it's Jack Cusak."

Inspector Jack Cusak is really quite a package. Let me give you the full tour. He's a large, rambling man, with thinning, gunmetal-gray hair, and a long, drooping mustache. His eyes are curtained by thick tufts of hair. He wears metal-framed glasses that look as though they were Army issued, and they are continually sliding down his rather bulbous nose. Though he is well over six feet tall, he walks in a stooped manner that makes him look a lot shorter. Someone had once described him as "being the kind of guy who could find a way to hate anyone."

Whitman rushed over to talk to him.

"You know the policeman, I take it?" Jane said.

"Only too well."

I filled her in on some of Cusak's peculiarities.

A crowd was gathering and there was some nervous muttering.

"Do you have any idea what happened?" Jane said.

"Not a clue. It must have something to do with Martel. I haven't seen him since before the card game broke up."

"I'm going to mingle and see what I can find out," she said.

Cusak and Whitman conversed for a while, then Cusak walked up a half dozen of the stairs leading to the second floor.

"Ladies and gentlemen," he said in a voice cured by a lifelong whiskey rash, "there has been a robbery committed. Mr. Martel has been injured. If you would be good enough to give your names, and any information you have to the uniformed police officers, it would be appreciated. As soon as you have identified yourselves, you're free to leave. Thank you very much."

For Cusak, it was a pretty elegant speech. He marched over to me, speared me with his ball-bearing eyes, and said, "You stick around, asshole."

So much for elegance.

Jane came by a few minutes later, hovering over a shiny metal gurney holding the blanketed body of Lionel Martel. There was a bandage on his head and his left hand was encased in some bloody towels.

As the ambulance attendants maneuvered the gurney toward the door, she came over to me, her lovely face creased with concern.

"He's going to be all right. He's got a bump on his head and a bad cut on his hand. They're going to take him to the Mt. Zion Hospital to check him out. Tony is going to drive me to the hospital, then I'm going to the paper to do the story." She consulted the slim gold watch on her wrist. "I should be able to get it in the morning edition." She placed her hand on my shoulder and smiled. "Do you think you could stick around and pump the police for me? Find out just what the hell is going on? Then call me at the paper. Then maybe we can have breakfast."

"Ah, breakfast. I knew there had to be some reward for my labors. Okay. But who the hell is Tony?"

She pointed a long, red fingernail at the tall, debonair gentleman I'd seen her dancing with earlier.

"Oh, him," I said with little enthusiasm. "Okay, take off, I'll stick around and see what I can come up with."

I watched Jane and Tony stop to identify themselves to the uniformed officers guarding the front door. Tony was somewhere in his fifties, the stiff-back, stand-erect type. He had a British look about him, like one of those lancers who would saddle up and go out and kill a few hundred thuggees in the name of the Queen. "Good man, Tony. Can always count on him in a pinch, eh, what, old chap?"

Jane and I saw a lot of each other. We also, by mutual agreement, saw others. Her one and only experience with marriage was a disaster, and one she was not anxious to repeat. So we'd meet almost daily for a couple of weeks, and then maybe not again for a couple of weeks. It was a wonderful arrangement, and while I heartily agreed with it, it in no way stopped me from hoping that the carefully groomed thatch of silver-gray hair on top of Tony's head was a toupee and would slip off during their ride to the hospital, and that his teeth slept in another room than he did, and that he was impotent. Nothing serious, just a few slight imperfections.

I found a comfortable chair, helped myself to some coffee, and sat and watched the parade of policemen march by. The crime lab came and went, and most of the uniformed boys were gone when Inspector Jack Cusak summoned me.

An inspector in the San Francisco Police Department ranks just above a sergeant, and below a lieutenant. At one time it was an appointive position, or "juice job." You had to know someone to get it. Later they opened it to one of man's worst creations, a civil service examination. Cusak had got it on "juice," though I was never able to find out just who his juice was.

You know those movies where the commissioner, or captain, calls in the lieutenant and tells him if he doesn't crack this case in so many hours, "I'll kick you back to patrolman and have you back walking a beat"? Pure movie magic. Once you're appointed up a rank in real civil service, it's your property, and to lose it you'd have to do something really stupid, like kick the mayor in the ass. In front of witnesses. An increasingly wishful proposition considering the type of mayors we've been getting lately.

So, once you're in, you're in. There wasn't much chance of Cusak's screwing up because he never really did anything. He went to the Hall of Justice in the morning, took off his jacket, loosened his tie, took a couple of day-old doughnuts out of his paper bag, read the newspaper, scrupulously avoided answering the phone, and turned a deaf ear as long as possible to anyone calling out his name. He was the epitome of a civil service career man; "they can't fuck you if you just don't do anything."

Cusak bounced around from one detail to another on about a yearly basis: General Works, Homicide, Burglary, Sex Crimes, Fraud, Missing Persons, Robbery, Narcotics, Vice. He's seen them all, leaving not a visible footprint in the sands of crime.

Unfortunately he was now working Aggravated Assault. It might be the perfect position for him. He could aggravate anyone.

He stomped over to my chair, glowered down at me, and said, "This way, Polo." He had a way of drawing out his vowels that made my name come out PowLow.

I followed his hulking back down the same hallway I'd followed Jane just a few hours earlier to the poker game. We made a left turn before getting to the game room. Cusak held the mirrored door open for me, slamming it shut behind me.

The room was small, all dark cherrywood. Two walls were lined with books that looked as if they were picked because their covers matched the wood in the room. A leather couch in saddle brown stood against the far wall. A brass armchair, the seat and back covered with what looked like real tiger skin, sat in front of a richly carved cherrywood desk.

Cusak flopped into a padded leather executive chair behind the desk while I edged my way cautiously onto the tiger-skinned job.

On top of the desk was a large platter of shrimp.

Cusak helped himself to two of the shrimp, somehow got both of them in his mouth at the same time, and between bites, said, "All right, Polo. Just what the hell happened here tonight?"

"I was hoping you'd tell me, Inspector."

He snorted and went for more shrimp. "How'd you get in?"

I looked confused. He paused, belched loudly, then said, "How the hell did you get into this party?"

"I was invited."

"By who?"

"Jane Tobin. A reporter for the *Bulletin*."

He wiped a hand across his lips and stared lovingly at the shrimp tray.

"She pay your way?" he asked.

"No, I paid."

His head bounced up, and his glasses slid down his nose. "I was told it cost a full five hundred clams to get in to this bullshit thing."

"You were told right."

The glasses moved slowly, millimeter by millimeter down his pocked nose. Just before they reached the tip, he used an index finger to push them up to the top again.

"I know you, Polo. You're a hustler. A wise guy. You quit the department and you did time in the federal slammer. You ain't the kind of guy who goes around spending half a thousand bucks just to get into some half-assed charity event to give more money to those homeless assholes. So why don't you save us both a lot of trouble and tell me just why the hell you ended up here tonight. And why the frog who throws the party just happens to have his head bashed in while you were here."

"By 'the frog,' I take it you mean Lionel Martel? How badly was he hurt?"

Cusak's tongue went fishing around his cheeks for parts of a missing shrimp. It took a full circle; first bulging out his left cheek, then under his mustache, then over to the right cheek, then under his lower lip before giving up.

"You know this Martel guy?" he said, stretching an arm out to the shrimp tray.

"Never met him before this evening."

"Talk to him?"

"We exchanged a few polite words, that was about it."

"Bullshit," he said, slamming a fist down on the desk hard enough to rattle the shrimp tray. "Roy Whitman told me you was in a poker game with him. What happened? He took you for some dough, you argued with him to get it back, and when he wouldn't come up with it, you knocked him over the head. That the way it went down?"

"I saw Whitman bob his head into the room when we were playing cards. He must have told you there were several other players. If you talk to them, you'll find out that Martel left the room before the game broke up. A waiter came in and told him he had a phone call. I never saw him after he left the table."

"You can prove that, I guess, huh, Polo?" Again with the Powlow.

"I don't think I have to, Cusak," I said, his name coming out as Cooosack. "I stayed around to talk to you as a professional courtesy, to help if I could. If you're going to act like an asshole, I'm walking right now."

He leaned back in his chair and belched again. Once a policeman knows that you don't have to talk to him if you don't want to, unless you have the proverbial "smoking gun" in your hand, they usually push off the bluff button and push on the charm button. Cusak was missing several buttons, the charm one especially.

"You getting wise with me, Polo? I could make it tough for you."

"You wouldn't know how, Cusak. Besides, I know who your juice was, and I know just how you used him to get where you are. So don't fuck with me."

He blinked rapidly several times. I never played an easier bluff. He leaned both elbows on the desk.

"Listen," he said, "I'm just trying to do my job." He shoved the tray toward me. "Have a shrimp."

"No, thanks. How badly was Martel injured?"

"Hard to say. Bump on the head. Bad cut. There was blood all over the place. Nothing life threatening."

"Anything stolen?"

He puckered out his lips, and his glasses started their long slide down his nose again. "That's what I'm trying to find out. There's all kinds of shit around this place worth stealing. But I'll have to wait until I talk to Martel to be sure. He said something to the first uniform on the scene about some missing paintings, but I won't get the details till I talk to him."

I pushed the shrimp tray back toward him. "What about Roy Whitman? Where was he when Martel was attacked?"

Cusak shrugged his shoulders. "Says he was all over the place. He's the one that found him on the floor and called us." He used a thumbnail to scratch his mustache. "Kinda funny, isn't it? You and Whitman. Both was fuzzes. Both of you have been in more than your share of shit, and both of you here when it went down."

"But I've never been here before, Inspector. I wouldn't know if there was anything worth stealing. If I were you, I'd talk to the waiter who told Martel about the phone call."

"Yeah, yeah," Cusak said, standing up. "I got all kinds of guys I got to talk to. You can take off, Polo. I know where I can find you if I need you."

Before I closed the door after myself, I took one final peek at Cusak. He was stuffing shrimp in a yellowish-looking pocket handkerchief.

I had the choice of calling and waiting for a cab, or bumming a ride. San Francisco is a bad cab town. They're like policemen, never around when you need them.

There were two black-and-whites parked next to each other outside Martel's house, one pulled into the curb, the other alongside on the street, facing in opposite directions so the drivers could talk to each other through the cars' windows.

It hadn't been too many years since I quit the department, but it seemed as if there were a complete changeover in personnel. At one time I thought I knew most of the force by sight. Not anymore.

I took the San Francisco Police Department's inspector's badge I had never bothered to turn in out of my pants pocket and flashed it at the driver of the car on the street.

"Any chance of getting a ride to North Beach?" I said. "Cusack is going to be tied up in there for another hour."

The uniformed cop was a young black woman. She eyed my tuxedo suspiciously.

"I was at the party," I said, "you can't get away from crime in this damn town anymore."

She smiled ruefully. "Hop in, Inspector."

We small-talked for the few minutes it took her to drive from the rarified atmosphere of Pacific Heights to my flats on Green Street.

I called Jane at the *Bulletin*.

"What have you got for me?" she asked right away.

"Not too much." I told her what little I had learned from Cusak. "How's Martel doing?"

"I'll tell you when you pick me up in half an hour," she said, hanging up before I could say anything else.

A half hour gave me enough time to get out of the tuxedo, take a quick shower, and change into cords, a turtleneck, and windbreaker.

The reason I didn't drive Jane to the party in my car, is my car. Jane hates it. Calls it the Polomobile. It's a three-year-old Ford sedan, with a suitable number of dents and scratches, blackwall tires, a big whip antenna, and a red light hanging down from the sun visor on the passenger side. A hand mike lies on the front seat, the cord harmlessly taped to bare metal under the dash. I keep a clipboard with a few wanted posters on the backseat. There's a .38 snubnose in a hollowed-out hole in the headrest. It looks exactly like an unmarked police car. It's not that I have any misspent feelings about leaving the department. The car has one vital function: It seldom gets tagged, no matter where I park it. When I do find a tag flopping under the windshield, it's usually blank. That's what cops do when they have to tag a row of cars and one belongs to a cop, or a guy who owns a delicatessen and passes out hams and turkeys around the holidays. Give the great unwashed the real citations, and "the boys" a blank piece of paper. Unjust you say? Not really. If they do tag a real honest-to-God unmarked car, the cop wouldn't pay the tag, it wouldn't make much sense. The city would be tagging itself. Besides, the officer could be on official business, chasing the bad guys, with no time to drive around and find a legal parking space. Unjust as far as I'm concerned? Probably so, but I plead insanity. Looking for a parking space in this town would drive anyone crazy.

Jane's car is a beauty, a little Chrysler convertible, red, with a white top. A convertible in San Francisco is about as useful as a mink coat in Hawaii. If the weather does happen to be nice enough to have the top down, you have to make sure you stay within viewing distance when you park, otherwise the seats will be missing when you go back for it.

I have a friend; bright guy in almost every way, but for some reason he bought himself a BMW convertible. He had the top ripped open three times by someone with a fondness for the car's radio and tape deck. Finally he got fed up. Whenever he parked, he put a sign in the car's window: THIS VEHICLE DOES NOT HAVE A RADIO OR TAPE DECK. Came back one night, and scrawled in heavy knife cuts on the canvas roof was a message: GET ONE ASSHOLE! Guy drives a Ford pickup truck now.

I only had to shoot the breeze with the security guard at the *Bulletin* for a few minutes before Jane came down from her office, looking tired and mad.

"God, I need a drink, and something to eat," she said once she was in the car.

"What's the matter. You miss the deadline?"

"No, no problem there, but Lionel Martel. That knock on the head must have really rattled him. He wouldn't talk to me at the hospital. Actually shouted to the doctors to have me removed."

She settled her head against the car's headrest, the one with the .38 inside it. "So it really wasn't much of a story, Nick." She swiveled her head and smiled sweetly. "I did give you a plug though: 'Noted San Francisco private investigator Nick Polo, who was in attendance at the charity ball, is assisting the police in their investigation.' How's that?"

"It will really endear me to Inspector Cusak. Just how hungry are you?"

She patted her stomach with both hands. "Absolutely starved. And I need a drink."

It was after three in the morning. Food was no problem, there were dozens of restaurants open. Booze was, though. The bars close at two in the morning, and about the only after-hours joints in town were the gambling dens in Chinatown or the whorehouses in the Tenderloin, neither of which I thought would appeal to Jane.

So that left the Produce Mart, a two-block area on Jerrold Street in the Bayview District. All the buildings were the same: two-story corrugated steel, painted, for some reason, turquoise and white, over loading docks five feet above street level. Dozens of trucks of all sizes were backed onto the loading docks. Big, dark men, their exhaled breath hanging like cigar smoke in the chill morning air, were loading and unloading crates of lettuce, potatoes, and onions. Open boxes of apples, oranges, grapefruit, pears, and other exotic fruits and vegetables were on display in the vendors' stalls.

I parked in front of a fire hydrant and led Jane into a coffee shop with a chipped black sign saying BEL'S on the plate-glass window. The place was jammed, and I grabbed Jane's elbow and guided her to an empty booth in the rear. There was a large, open kitchen off to the right, and the pungent aroma of coffee permeated the air.

Jane sank into the cracked imitation-leather seats and looked over her shoulder. Of the forty or so customers, she was the only woman. She started to unbutton her coat, then thought better of it.

"Why is it I have the feeling that Tony would have brought me to a place with tablecloths and champagne in buckets?" She took a long look over her shoulder. "This place is a gold mine," she said. "Who are all these people?"

"Produce men, restaurant owners, people who run the mom-and-pop grocery stores. Everyone from the Top of the Mark on down. They're buying the day's supplies. It's like this every morning." I waved toward the kitchen. "Hey, Joey. We both need a cba to start with."

The cook, a short, thick-shouldered man, waved back and relayed the order to a harried waitress.

"What's a cba?" Jane asked suspiciously.

"Coffee, brandy, and a touch of anisette. It's the official drink down here." I rubbed my hands together. "Just the thing for a cold morning."

The drinks were brought in heavy white mugs. Jane sipped at hers cautiously at first, decided she liked it, and took a deeper swallow.

The waitress hovered over us with a pencil and order pad. "*Costa te voretere di mangiare?*" she asked.

"Bring us two more of these in a few minutes, then we'll order," I said, then turned back to Jane and asked, "What happened to good old Tony?"

"After we left the hospital, he dropped me off at the paper." She arched an eyebrow at me. "I told him I'd be busy the rest of the morning. We've got a tentative date for dinner tomorrow. What I can't understand is the change in Lionel Martel."

"Under the circumstances, you can't expect him to be his usual charming self."

· She shook her head. "No, this was different, Nick. I mean, as soon as he saw me, he started screaming, "Get her out of here! Get her out of here!"

"Maybe he's just publicity shy."

She took a deep swallow from her mug. "I don't know. I wish you could have learned more from this Inspector Cusak."

The waitress came with two more drinks. "Are you ready to order now, Nick?"

"Okay. I'll have garlic sausage, eggs over easy, and toast."

"Make that two," Jane said, reaching for her fresh cba. "Didn't Cusak tell you anything about what was stolen?"

"Just what I told you. Apparently Martel told the first cop on the scene that some paintings were gone. He'll have to wait for Martel to tell him just what was taken."

"How about that other private investigator? The blond hunk. Did you talk to him?"

"Roy Whitman? We're not exactly on speaking terms. He wouldn't tell me anything. You, he'd talk to. In fact, if he thought you'd put his name in the paper, he'd be over to scrub your back, then your floors, and then do the windows."

"Then maybe I will talk to him," Jane said. "What is it between you two?"

"We worked together as patrolmen for a short while. Whitman was, probably still is, what I call a cripple picker. If he can find a weakness in anyone, he'll pick away at it till it breaks. He was a shakedown artist, the kind of guy who'd swipe a drunk's wallet, slip a ring off a stiff's finger. He also liked to push people around. Always people who were smaller than him, or drunk or drugged out of their skulls. We had a beef, or as they say in police jargon, an 'altercation' at Ingleside Station one night. He was pushing around some harmless drunk, 'Doorway Patty,' we always called him. Old Doorway was ahead of his time, a forerunner of today's homeless. He'd get drunk every night and wind up in some doorway on Mission Street. Whitman was cuffing him around for no good reason."

"So you and Whitman got into a fight?" she asked.

"Right in front of God, Doorway Patty, and the booking lieutenant."

Jane had already finished her second cba, so I signaled for another round.

"I know all about your quitting the department," she said, "but what about Whitman? Why'd he leave?"

"He squeaked out before he got canned. He was working with a burglary ring. He'd case places for them, set it up so he was on duty the night of the burglary. The DA thought he had Whitman dead to rights, but Whitman showed up in court looking like an altar boy. Broke down and cried on the stand. Somehow the jury went for it. They convicted his partners, who ended up in San Quentin. Whitman walked free."

The waitress came, balancing huge platters and two

more coffee mugs. The platters were covered with two thick garlic sausages, three sunny-side-up eggs, and mounds of cottage fries. Toast at Bel's was a quarter loaf of French bread, loaded with butter, garlic, and Parmesan cheese.

Jane's eyes widened as she looked at the food. "God, I'll never be able to eat all of this."

She came close. She cut into the egg with surgical care, watching the yolk yellow the plate and potatoes, then she unbuttoned her coat and rolled up her sleeves and dug in. The coat unbuttoning brought us a lot of attention, and guys I barely knew or hadn't seen in years came over to say hello and admire the view.

"Haven't you got any other ideas about the robbery?" Jane asked, working her way through the potatoes.

"If I were going to work on it, I'd check out the waiters. Especially the one who came and told Martel about the phone call. He looked like a waiter like Cusak looks like a ballet dancer."

"Did you tell Cusak about him?" she asked, blotting up the remains of the egg with a piece of toast.

"I mentioned something about waiters. I don't know if he'll follow through."

"You could, though," Jane said.

I popped a piece of garlic sausage in my mouth. "Why? Nothing in it for me."

"Don't you feel sorry for Lionel?"

"Very. I hope he doesn't end up suffering from amnesia. He owes me some money from the card game."

She stretched her foot across the table and ran it up my calf. "You know, Nick Polo, you made a very big mistake tonight."

"What was that?"

She smiled and kept running her foot up and down my leg. "You should have ordered something without garlic," she said with a polite little burp.

32

Things went on for what passed for normal the next couple of days. I did get a growling call from Cusak regarding my name's popping up in Jane's story on the robbery.

I worked on a couple of simple locate cases for some steady insurance company clients; good, solid, boring, well-paying cases, locating witnesses to a boating accident that had taken place on San Francisco Bay four years earlier.

I was finishing up the reports on my word processor when the phone rang. A deep, cultured voice asked for Mr. Polo.

"Speaking."

"Mr. Polo, this is Claude Martel. I would very much appreciate it if I could see you this afternoon."

My afternoon schedule consisted of a possible nap or a trip to the racetrack. "I think I can squeeze you in, Mr. Martel."

"Wonderful. Shall we say two o'clock, at my home?"

I put on my dark blue clients' suit, and at just a minute or two before two I was once again at the Martel residence in Pacific Heights. Sounds impressive, Pacific Heights, though no one really knows how it got its name, since the view isn't of the Pacific Ocean but of the Bay. After the big earthquake of 1906, all the shakers and movers in town moved out of the devastated area of Nob Hill to the high ground and built their new mansions.

This time the front door was opened by a tall, thin, serious-looking man in a dark charcoal suit.

"Nick Polo to see Mr. Martel."

"You are expected, sir. Right this way please."

The floor of the front entrance had been covered up by a rug on my last visit. It was bare now, the flooring a swirling pattern of exotic hardwoods. I stopped to admire the work that went into creating it. It made you want to take off your shoes and shuffle across.

I followed behind. He walked with a rigid back and his arms straight down at his sides, head tilted slightly back. He had probably practiced long and hard by balancing a book on his noggin. We went up the stairway to the second floor.

"If you'll wait, I'll inform Mr. Martel that you are here, sir," said my tour guide.

The room was all royal blue and glass. The couches and floor were of a deep royal blue. The walls were more of the same blue, with one wall entirely of glass shelving holding crystal bowls and animal sculptures. Track lighting hung around the border of a panel-mirrored ceiling. A glass coffee table, three feet by six, sat in the middle of the room. I felt as though I were standing in a swimming pool looking up at the reflections.

"Ah, Mr. Polo. So good of you to come," said the gray-haired man entering the room. There was a resemblance between Claude and Lionel Martel. The senior was shorter, his hair completely gray, but he had the same droopy eyelids his son had. He also had a handshake that would have done justice to a stevedore. He was dressed in casual elegance: gray slacks, an opened-neck white dress shirt with a black silk scarf knotted around his neck, and a camel-hair sport coat. He looked to be in his seventies. You almost have to be that old, or a member of the British aristocracy, to get away with the scarf-around-the-neck look. He was carrying a thin, pigskin briefcase.

"Please sit down, sir. Would you care for something to drink?"

"No, I'm fine, Mr. Martel. How can I help you?"

He settled himself into the blue couch. "I would like to hire you to help me get back what was taken from my home the other night." He took a long, very dark cigar from his jacket pocket, lit it with a gold lighter, and inhaled it as if it were a cigarette. "The newspaper said you were working with the police."

"An exaggeration, Mr. Martel. The lady who wrote the story is a friend. She thought the story might do me some good."

"And did it?"

"No. Especially not with the police."

He puffed away on his cigar. "I have spoken to Inspector Cusak. One of the reasons for my success is that I have been able to evaluate people quite quickly. My opinion of Cusak is that he is a fool."

"You wouldn't find too many people who would argue with you on that."

He leaned forward. "Since you were once a policeman, of the same rank as Inspector Cusak, tell me, what are the chances of his being replaced by another investigator?"

"Slim. Unless someone with a lot of pull went over his head and demanded the change."

He nodded his head and leaned back again. "I would not want Cusak replaced. I'm quite happy that he is in charge of the police department's investigation. Lionel has been a disappointment. He should never have opened the vault. Then he made that unfortunate statement about a robbery. But that has been corrected. As far as the police are concerned, nothing was stolen." He carefully crossed one leg over the other, smoothing out the pants crease on the top leg. "My evaluation of you, Mr. Polo, is just the opposite of the one I made of Cusak." He snapped open his briefcase and pulled out some papers, put on a pair of horn-rimmed glasses, and began reading. "Nicholas Polo. Retired early from the police department with the rank of inspector. You worked in various departments, and one time were successful in locating some very valuable paintings taken from the Museum of Modern Art. You have a good knowledge of art and also have connections with criminal elements in town."

I was wondering where he got his information. My knowledge of art stemmed from being dragged to museums on weekends by my mother. Later, I found myself going on my own. I could identify the styles of certain artists, but wouldn't know a forged work from a real one. As for finding the paintings taken from the museum, that was the result of a tip from a disgruntled thief who didn't think he got his fair share after seeing the bloated estimates printed in the newspapers. As for connections with criminal elements in town, my uncle was a small-time bookie, but if Martel wanted to think I was an art expert and had dinners with Mafia dons, why spoil his fun?

"Your parents died," he continued, "and you inherited a little money and a small piece of property." He put the papers down and looked at me. "There's nothing here to say exactly why you left the department. You're still a young man."

"It wasn't fun anymore," I said.

He waited for a further explanation. There wasn't one.

Martel went back to his papers. "You were arrested for failure to report the recovery of a sum of half a million dollars, said sum retrieved from a drug dealer of some sort."

The worst sort. He was a client of an attorney I was working for at the time. I took the money to the attorney, who took half, told me to keep the rest, then suddenly got panicky and turned me in.

Martel's voice droned on. "You served time in Lompoc

Federal Prison, were released, and have continued your work as a private investigator. You are described as hardworking and dependable."

"By whom?"

Martel dropped the papers back into the briefcase. "In my position, Mr. Polo, I deal with attorneys. Dozens of them. I asked them to check you out. They don't seem to feel comfortable unless they speak to other attorneys. They found someone who knows you. It was he who described you as hardworking and dependable. The other material was developed through newspaper stories, I gather."

"Who was the attorney who gave me the passing marks?"

Martel frowned and dug back into the briefcase. "A Mr. James Biernat."

Biernat was a topflight defense counsel. I'd have to thank him for the plug.

"I'd like you to go to work for me, Mr. Polo. You're the right man for the job, you're . . ." He waved his hand over his head trying to pull the right word out of the air. *"Un peu louche,"* he finally said.

"Huh?" was my clever response.

He spelled it out for me. "It means honest, but not stupidly so. There is one condition, however." He paused to take some more puffs on his cigar. "The reporter, Miss Tobin. She has been calling incessantly. I don't want to talk to her. I don't want my son to talk to her. And if you do go to work for me, I would not want you to give her any information whatsoever as to just what you are doing for me."

"That's not a problem. Jane's a friend, but if I work for you, what's between us is exactly that. Just between us. Just what is it that you want me to do for you, Mr. Martel?"

"I want what was taken from this house. I want it very badly. I am willing to pay for it. And I will pay you quite well, too, sir." He tapped some cigar ash into a crystal ashtray shaped like an upended turtle.

"What exactly was taken, Mr. Martel?"

"Some paintings. Valuable paintings."

"Were they insured?"

He waved an elegant hand at the ceiling. "No, these particular paintings could not be insured. They are invaluable. I must have them back, I will do anything to have them back," he said with an air of confession. "And I do not want the police involved in any way."

"I'll do what I can," I said. "Do you have photographs of the paintings?"

He jabbed his cigar out in the ashtray. There was still a good seven or eight inches left on it, and it looked as if it cost a buck an inch. "No. Those won't be needed. I would like you to somehow get the word out that I want the paintings back. What do you suggest?"

"When pieces are stolen from a museum or a private collection, they're usually too well-known to peddle on the street. They're usually sold right back to the museum or collector they were stolen from in the first place. Is that what we're talking about here?"

His hand went inside his jacket and came out with a checkbook, then dipped back in again for a pen. No cheap ballpoint for Martel. This was a Montblanc gold fountain pen.

"No, not exactly," Martel said, balancing the checkbook on his briefcase. "But you're right. I expect to be contacted and offered the paintings back. For a price of course. Once contact is made, I will get in touch with you, and you can negotiate the return of the paintings. Is that satisfactory?" he asked, ripping out a check with a flourish and handing it to me. "In the meantime, I want you to nose around, see what you can find out."

His handwriting was a bit sloppy, but I had no trouble in reading the figure: five thousand dollars.

"That's a lot of money for someone who may be nothing more than a messenger boy."

He smiled widely, showing a string of teeth that were too good to be true. "I'm sure you will earn your money, Mr. Polo. And there will be a substantial bonus if things work out well. Do you have any suggestions as to what we could do to speed things up?"

"I'd like to talk to Lionel."

Martel shook his head sadly. "Lionel should never have allowed that foolish affair to take place here." He slapped his hand down on the couch cushion. "Absolutely never should have allowed it. Lionel spends most of his time at his apartment." His hand went back to his jacket pocket for his pen. He wrote down Lionel's address and phone number. "I'll call and advise him you'll be contacting him. Anything else?"

"I'd like a list of everyone who attended the charity ball, and also a list of your employees and the people who worked here that night. Who hired the caterer?"

"Lionel." He sighed and took a deep breath. "Don't worry about the employees. We haven't time for that."

"Have you spoken to Roy Whitman?" I said.

"Several times." He sighed again. "Lionel had employed him previously on something personal. I don't know what it was. I imagine it had to do with some girl Lionel was having problems with. Whitman seems incompetent. An amateur." He put a little French backspin on the word.

Score one for Claude Martel. He was good at evaluating people.

"The waiter who came and called your son to the telephone. He definitely didn't look like the waiter type."

"You mentioned this to the police?" Martel asked.

"Not directly. I just told Cusak he should check the help."

Martel brought his hands together and rubbed them together briskly. "Good, very good, Mr. Polo. Do whatever you think necessary to identify this man. But remember, no police. Use your own sources. I still have my galleries, and solid connections in the art world. If any one of the paintings turns up on the legitimate market, I will know."

He stood up and walked over and patted me on the back, a coach sending his second-string quarterback into the game in the last quarter. "Yes, I think you are the man to help me get those paintings back."

8

Martel gave me a final handshake. The same tall, dour dude who had let me in was ready to escort me back out. We were halfway down the stairs when an attractive woman, somewhere in her late thirties or early forties, came in the front door. We met at the bottom of the stairs. Her hair was streaked in blond and beige. She was wearing a smart-looking red outfit, skirt and jacket. The jacket had big red buttons that started at her shoulder and went all the way down the left side. Her shoes were a matching red, as was her lipstick. She had a slight overbite, something some men, myself included, find erotic. She looked like someone who spent a lot of time and money at staying beautiful. It was time and money well spent.

"Hello. Do I know you?" she said. There was a slight French accent.

"I haven't had the pleasure. Nick Polo."

"I'm Denise Martel. I guess you were here to see my husband."

"Good guess."

She extended her hand in a way that made me think she wanted it kissed, rather than shaken. I settled for a polite shake. She had soft hands, and long nails. It might have been my imagination, but the nails seemed to drag along my palm as we separated hands.

"A pleasure to meet you, Mr. Polo." She smiled brightly, flaunting that damn overbite. "Is my husband upstairs?"

"Yes, he was a minute ago."

She nodded and headed for the stairs. My escort coughed loudly and held the door wide open.

As I drove back to my place, I thought about Claude Martel. He was well satisfied with Cusak handling the case, because Cusak would get nowhere. Especially with no cooperation from Lionel Martel. And I bet that Lionel did just what his father wanted him to do. What was so mysterious about the missing paintings? If they were so damn valuable, he'd have them photographed, catalogued, x-rayed. Insurance? Hell, I was having trouble paying my car insurance. What would it cost to insure "invaluable paintings"?

Jane Tobin was coming over for dinner, so I parked the car in the garage and walked down Green Street to do the shopping.

North Beach was once almost a hundred percent Italian. It's changing rapidly. Chinatown, for which Broadway was once a firm borderline, now spilled into the Beach and in a few more years would probably engulf it. Some of the old *paesanos* are finding the prices offered for their little houses and stores just too much to turn down. The little espresso shops and trattorias are slowly giving way to brightly decorated spots offering dim sum, Hunan, and even sushi. Store windows that used to be filled with salamis, *focaccia*, pastas, and exotic-looking cans of olive oil, now featured rows of those beautiful reddish-gold ducks hanging by their necks, and dozens of wide-eyed fish displayed on trays of ice. If you enjoyed cooking and eating, North Beach was close to paradise.

My first stop was the Bank of America, where I deposited Martel's check, then I went to Little City Meats and picked up some *vitellone*, Italian veal at its best, then to Iacopi's for some house-made prosciutto and *tortas*, next to Stella Pastry for a *sacripantina*, an absolutely obscene sponge-cake concoction filled with zabaglione and liqueurs. Then to the Italian-French Bakery for a nice crusty loaf of sourdough bread, and a final stop at the Chinese grocery store for a casaba melon. A little more complicated than plowing through your neighborhood supermarket, but well worth the effort.

I was lugging my brown bags up Green Street when I saw something that made me almost drop everything on my feet. Mrs. Damonte, my one and only tenant, was standing in front of my flats, armed as usual, a broom in one hand, a garden hose in the other. She was talking to a man, and she was smiling. The fact that she was talking to someone was strange enough. She spoke Italian. I'm sure she understood English, but her spoken vocabulary was limited: "nopa," her usual negative response to almost any question; "shita," when she found a snail in her vegetable garden, or when she paid her rent; and "bingo," something she constantly complained about not having the opportunity to say often enough.

Mrs. D. would have had to stand on her toes and stretch to reach five feet, and since she was somewhere in her eighties, she didn't stretch too often. Smiling was something she didn't do very often either. The gentleman she was conversing with had his back to me. As I got closer, I could hear them. My command of Italian is limited, but I could make out something about Genoa. Mrs. D. was Genovese, a tribe she considered far superior to any other Italian community. She came from a little village that had also sent Dominico Ghirardelli, the Chocolate King, to America. Giannini, the founder of Bank of America, was also from Genoa, a long way from the hills of Sicily, where my distant ancestors roamed.

43

She dropped the smile from her face when she saw me come up on them.

The man turned to face me. He was short, somewhat stocky, with thick black hair combed straight back from his face. His nose had a slight hook to it. His eyes were dark and he had the kind of beard that needed more than one shave a day. He was wearing a well-cut gray suit, white shirt, solid-black silk tie, and highly polished black shoes. He could get away with the plain tie, due to the quality of the suit. He smiled, offered to shake my hand, saw mine were full of groceries, then said, "Mr. Polo? How do you do. My name is Gene Lembi. Can I give you a hand with those?"

"No, thanks. What can I do for you?"

He made a bow in Mrs. D.'s direction. "I was just talking to Mrs. Damonte. She said you should be home in a little while. It is a business matter. If you could spare me just a few minutes."

He had a guttural, mixed accent, a little French, and a little Italian, a little of something I couldn't place.

"Sure," I said. "Come on inside." Anyone who could charm Mrs. Damonte needed a second look.

He had a limp and followed me stiff-legged up the terrazzo steps, still damp and smelling of Pine Sol from Mrs. D.'s scrubbing. She went through Pine Sol like Aunt Jemima goes through syrup.

Lembi took one of my bags while I opened the door. I carried the groceries into the kitchen, and when I got back to the front room, Lembi was standing with his head tilted to one side, studying the record albums and compact-disc packs stacked on one wall.

"You like the jazz, Mr. Polo?" he said.

"Yes. Now what exactly is it you want, Mr. Lembi?"

He took a thin, black leather folder from his suit jacket and flipped it open. There was a red-and-green-bordered card that showed Gene Lembi was an agent for Interpol. The International Criminal Police Organization. I had seen some fancy ID in my day, all kinds of badges, and FBI and CIA cards, but this was my first look at someone who claimed to be with Interpol.

"Very impressive," I said. "But I know a shop down on Market Street that sells those for five bucks."

He didn't appear offended. "I can give you the telephone number of our National Central Bureau in Washington. Or you can call the local office of Alcohol, Tobacco and Firearms."

I didn't know a lot about Interpol, other than that most of what you saw on TV was highly exaggerated. I did know that their headquarters were in France, and that most of the non-Communist countries in the world were members. I also knew that an Interpol agent has no actual powers of arrest, or search or seizure. They have to work with the local cops if they're going to be around when any arrests are made. Their main connection in America is through the federal bureau ATF, Alcohol, Tobacco and Firearms.

"I'll accept your credentials, Mr. Lembi." I looked at my watch. It was after five. "How about a drink?"

His was scotch and water, no ice. I settled for a glass of white wine. He made himself at home at the kitchen table, one arm hooked over the back of the chair, his legs crossed, one foot dangling, while I made the drinks.

He took a deep sip of his drink, then said, "I wanted to talk to you about the robbery at the Martel house."

"Why?" I asked, dropping into the chair directly across from him.

"Mr. Martel is of some interest to us."

"He's an interesting guy."

One of his eyebrows arched up, the other dropped down. "And a new client of yours?"

"What makes you think that?" My first thought was that Interpol was working with someone very heavy in the law enforcement field if they could bug the home of someone like Claude Martel.

"Just a guess," Lembi said. "I know you were at the party when young Martel was assaulted." He paused, his eyes focusing right into mine. "And that you were at his home this very afternoon."

"If you're trying to impress me, Lembi, you've succeeded. I'm flattered to think that Interpol thinks enough of me to have me tailed around town."

The eyes lowered. "We were not tailing you. But as I said before, we do have an interest in Claude Martel."

"Enough of an interest to have his house watched?"

"What do you know of Claude Martel?"

"Just that he seems very rich. And that his wife is very beautiful, and that his son had an unusual accident."

He went through the eyebrow routine again. "You know Mrs. Martel?"

"Just met her this afternoon. Come on, Lembi, quit sparring around. Ask what you want to ask. I've got company coming for dinner."

"Ah, yes. I wouldn't like to upset your dinner." He took a long swallow of his drink, then leaned forward on the table. "I would like to tell you a story. It won't take long."

I never met a cop who could tell a short story, so I got up and freshened our drinks.

"Are you much of a student of World War Two?" Lembi asked.

"I saw every episode of *War and Remembrance*."

He looked confused.

"I know a little," I said, "but I'm sure you're going to broaden my education."

"Hitler had a special force known as the Kunstschutz, which was in charge of confiscating works of art. Anything that they could get their hands on, by any means they chose to use. Anything of value was fair game: paintings, sculpture, jewelry, old coins, rare books. Tapestries, even chalices were taken from churches. Works by all the great masters— Rembrandt, Botticelli, Picasso, Rubens, Chagall, Vandyke—

all disappeared from the churches, synagogues, and the homes of Jews.

"There was so much art. But the German high command wasn't satisfied with the share of the loot they were getting, so Martin Borman had one of his flunkies, Alfred Rosenberg, create a fun little group called the Einsatzstab Reichsleiter Rosenberg, the ERR. So now the art that didn't find its way to Hitler ended up in the hands of Borman, Goering, Goebbels, the Gestapo leaders, and even with some of the German bankers and industrialists who were favorites of the Third Reich.

"These thugs could just go wherever they wanted and take whatever they saw fit. There was Goebbels, surely the most prolific 'spin master' the world has ever seen. It frightens me to think what he could do if he were alive today. He proclaimed that great art was the legal property of Germany, because art owed its inspiration to its Teutonic origins."

Lembi made interlocking rings on the kitchen table with the bottom of his glass of scotch.

"Very methodical people, the Nazis," he continued. "They made sure they kept detailed ledgers on all their operations, be it loading Jews into ovens, or stealing art. According to their own files, and we don't believe we found all of them, there were over ten million works confiscated. Ten million, from France, Russia, Belgium, Denmark, Poland, Norway. Everywhere they went, they looted."

"This is all fascinating stuff, Lembi," I said, "but what has it to do with a guy named Nick Polo?"

He held up a palm. "Patience. I'm coming to that." He went back to making circles with his glass. "When the war started going badly for the Germans, they started shipping their stolen treasures out of the country. Some made it, most did not. They hid them in old buildings, caves in the mountains, salt mines. We found whole trainloads of the stuff. Your president Roosevelt appointed members of the Metropolitan Museum to head up a staff called the MFAA. Monuments, Fine Arts and Archives. They were part of the Office of Strategic Services, the forerunner of the CIA. Their job was to find the looted art and return it to its rightful owners. Of course, most of the owners had met their fate in the Nazi gas chambers. But they did turn up quite a bit. A Rubens was found in a former Gestapo office. It had been used for a dart board. It's impossible to imagine how many masterpieces were simply burned or thrown away. Horror stories abound of houses ransacked, the sculpture used for target practice, paintings ripped from their frames and used to wrap sandwiches or bottles of stolen wine.

"The OSS didn't have much use for the MFAA boys. Thought they were sissies. Which didn't bother the MFAA people at all. They were left on their own. They had free rein, and many of them did a good job, I'm sure. But just as the OSS had to deal with ex-Nazi spies to get information, the MFAA dealt with the same Nazi officials who had confiscated the art in the first place, and the sympathetic dealers who had cooperated with the Nazis, told them just who had what, and what it was worth.

"The MFAA started working sometime in 1943 and lasted until 1951. Hundreds of thousands of works of art passed through their hands. It must have been tempting, no? A lone MFAA investigator finds a painting. He alone determines if it is really a work of art. Its value had to be estimated as at least five thousand dollars to qualify. If it was worth less than that, it simply wasn't considered art. And what did these MFAA men do if they determined that a certain painting or print or piece of sculpture was not a work of art? It was a simple matter to have a package sent back home through the mails, or shipped home with a friend going back to the United States." Lembi picked up his drink and took a long swallow. "There were fewer than a hundred and fifty members of the MFAA, and Claude Martel was one of them."

Gene Lembi sat there waiting for me to make a state-ment. He was a patient man. Most good cops are. My options were either to outwait him or say something to get the ball rolling again. Since Jane Tobin was due to be knock-ing on my door any minute, I let Lembi win his waiting game by saying something intelligent.

"So?" I said.

"If I tell you a story, can I count on your not passing on the information to Claude Martel?"

"Martel hired me to do a job," I said.

"After you hear this story, you may want to terminate your employment."

This was getting too deep for me. I could box Inspector Jack Cusak around all I wanted, but Lembi was in the big leagues; Interpol was well connected with the other alpha-bet-soup boys: FBI, CIA, NSA, and ATF. Heavyweights, who could make things unpleasant for you. "All right," I said, "whatever you say stays with me."

"Claude Martel was born in France. He came to Amer-ica with his family when he was eleven years old. His father had a small art gallery in New York. Claude worked for the Metropolitan Museum. When he was drafted, he was noth-

ing more than a private, attached to the signal corps. Someone at the Metropolitan remembered him when MFAA was
formed. He was perfect for them: young, intelligent, with an
impeccable art background. He naturally welcomed the
transfer. He spent over three years in Europe with MFAA,
Mr. Polo. Shortly after he returned, his father died. Claude
took over their art gallery. The gallery grew enormously during the next few years. Martel became quite wealthy. He
expanded his business from the art world into real estate,
made a fortune, and eventually moved his headquarters to
San Francisco."

"So what you're saying is that Martel built his empire
on some artwork he stole, confiscated, or just stumbled
across while he was in the Army," I said.

Lembi examined his carefully manicured fingernails.
"Things have not been going very well for Claude Martel as
of late. He overextended himself in some business ventures.
He has spent a lot of time in Europe the past few weeks.
Europe is still the art capital of the world, though it's the
Japanese who have been sending the prices up so much
lately. While he was in Brussels, a Chagall surfaced on the
market. The painting had not been seen in almost fifty years.
While he was in Paris, two Picassos, long thought to have
ended up in Russian hands were sold. A Vandyke was sold at
the same time Claude Martel was in London. All of these
paintings went very quickly, for enormous sums." Lembi
looked up from his nails and smiled. "Not as much as they
would have sold for at auction at Christie's. No, then there
would have been a lot of curiosity about just how and why
they had suddenly appeared. There were rumors that other
paintings, a Brueghel and even a Renoir, were being sold on
the *marché gris,* the gray market."

"Can you prove Martel was selling them?" I asked.

He gave me a Gallic shrug of his shoulders. "No. We
thought we might be on to something just recently in Paris,
but Martel suddenly bolted back to America when he heard
what had happened to his son."

I stood up and tied on an apron. "Just what do you want of me, Lembi?"

He scraped his chair back and reached for his wallet, the one with the fancy ID. "Here," he said, handing me a small piece of paper. "I can be reached at that number. There is a large reward. Very large, for the return of these works of art."

"And you think that the attack on Lionel Martel had something to do with all of this old OSS or MFAA stuff?"

"Do you know what actually happened to Lionel Martel, Mr. Polo?"

"I know he bumped his head. Must have been a pretty good rap. He apparently thought something was stolen. Turns out nothing was taken."

Lembi drew a deep breath. "I see. Your sources disappoint me, Mr. Polo, but thank you for your time, and the drinks."

When I opened the front door to let Lembi out, there stood Jane Tobin, her finger poised over the doorbell.

"No, thanks," I said, patting Lembi on the back. "I already have enough insurance, but thank you anyway."

Lembi gave Jane a polite nod and limped down the steps.

"Who the hell was that?" Jane asked, handing me her coat. "And don't say he was selling insurance. He had *cop* written all over him."

"You're losing your touch. He was way too well dressed for a cop, darling. How about making us a martini while I get started with dinner?"

I went down the back steps to Mrs. Damonte's garden, picked enough lettuce for a salad, some tomatoes, string beans, and rosemary.

While Jane washed the vegetables I snuck into my office, paged through the directory for the local number of the Alcohol, Tobacco and Firearms bureau. It was the same number Lembi had given me. I gave them a call.

A bored young voice came on the line and pronounced, "ATF."

I put a bit of a brogue in my voice and said, "Gene Lembi, please?"

"Who, sir?"

"Gene Lembi. He's with Interpol. I was told I could contact him through your office."

"Hold on, please."

I followed her orders, and in a minute or so a booming male voice came on the line. "Robinson here, how can I help you?"

"Robinson, how are you? This is Inspector Mike Wilcox, San Francisco Police Department. I was trying to get in touch with Gene Lembi. Interpol guy, was by here this morning."

"Lembi? I never heard of him. I'll have to check him out. What's your number?"

That's the problem with the telephone. You can be anyone you want and pump out a lot of information from people, but if they want to call you back with the information, you're stuck. Give them your real number, and if they check it out because the information you're trying to get isn't the type that is available to the ordinary citizen, you could get into some trouble. Give them a phony number, and you don't get what you're after. I gave Robinson the number for the Burglary Detail at the Hall of Justice, then said, "Robinson. I think I met you at a seminar once. You were with Stan Cordes, weren't you?"

"You know Stan?" Robinson asked.

"Oh, yeah. For a long time." At least long enough to see his name in the papers for the past few years, listing him as the head of the local Federal Bureau of Investigation office. When federal cops aren't trying to increase their budgets, they spend a lot of time at seminars, so it was a good bet that Robinson had attended a few. Also a good bet he either knew Cordes or at least did some discreet ass-kissing when the occasion arose. If none of the above were true, I'd have to hang up fast before Robinson ran a trace on the call.

"Yeah, I remember you, Wilcox. How's things? What detail you with now?"

"Burglary."

"Yeah. Okay, hang on. I'll see what I can find out about this Lembi guy."

I stared nervously at my watch's second hand. If Robinson kept me on hold over a minute, I'd have to hang up. The danger of his tracing the call and a charge of impersonating an officer wasn't worth the risk for the little information I was digging for.

Robinson popped back on the line in fifty-two seconds. "I don't know what Lembi's working on, Wilcox. He's listed as in the area, no special case. Want me to have him call you?"

"Yeah, fine."

"I'll put a message in for him. Take care."

Well, now at least I knew that Lembi was a legitimate Interpol agent.

Jane pecked away with questions about my guest while she made the drinks. She gave up by the time the salad was made.

The veal turned out better than I had expected since my mind was working overtime, trying to fend off Jane's questions about Lembi and trying to pick her brain about Lionel Martel.

We were on espresso and the *sacripantina* when the phone rang. It was Claude Martel.

"Come quickly," Martel said. "Contact has been made."

10

Claude Martel opened the door himself this time.

"Come in, come in," he said gruffly. "Follow me."

Following people around the Martel place was becoming a habit. We went down a hallway that was new to me, and into a large room dominated by an ornately carved Oriental desk. A fireplace surrounded by glazed Moroccan tiles sat in one corner. Two other walls were covered with framed photographs. The fourth wall showed the outside steel door of a safe, the walk-in kind you see in a bank, with a combination lock-and-wheel door opener. The big label on the door showed HITCHCOCK VAULT COMPANY. I knew the brand well from my time in the burglary detail. Top of the line, no way to finesse those babies. If you tried to blow it open, most of the house would fall down around it.

Half a dozen chairs were set around the desk. Roy Whitman was sprawled in one of them. He was wearing a ruffled tuxedo shirt, white, with little black studs and cuff links. His pants were blue jeans, the shoes lizard-skin cowboy jobs. A battered leather bomber jacket hung over the back of his chair. He had an "I know something you don't know" look on his face.

The desk held a round, glass cigar humidor, and two

phones, one red and one white. A small black box, the size of a five-pound box of candy, lay between the phones. The name EVALUATOR was stenciled on the box. It was one of the new microprocessors that continuously checks the phone line for the presence of a tap. It works by taking an electronic fingerprint of the phone line voltage and characteristics. Any kind of tap on the line and the machine warns you right away of the condition change. Even tells you if the tap is set up in series or parallel. Ain't science grand?

"Whitman," Martel said, walking behind the desk and sitting down. "Tell Polo about the call."

"A man called me. Said that he had some property belonging to Mr. Martel. He told me to tell Mr. Martel that he wanted to return the property, but that he thought that he deserved a proper reward."

"'Proper reward,'" I said. "Those his exact words?"

Whitman nodded his head. "Yep, exactly what he said."

"Where'd he call you?"

"At my office. About an hour ago."

"You were working late," I said.

Whitman smiled wearily. "It's the nature of the business. You have to be available at all hours. You should know that, Nick."

I couldn't argue with him there. "Why do you think he called you, instead of Mr. Martel, Roy?"

Whitman ran a heavy hand across his chin. "I don't know. I guess he knew I was handling security for Lionel Martel. He probably wanted a middleman so he wouldn't have to deal with Mr. Martel directly."

"What else did he say?"

Whitman turned so he was facing Martel. "He said he would turn over one of the items, to show good faith. If you were happy with that one item, he would negotiate a price for the return of the rest."

"When is all of this supposed to take place?" I asked.

Whitman said, "He told me to see Mr. Martel right away. That he'd call me at Martel's place."

Martel opened the humidor on his desk, took out one of those midget-league-bat-sized cigars, and said, "So now we wait."

The gentleman who had let me into the house earlier in the day brought in a tray with small, crust-free sandwiches and coffee. Right behind him was a tall, dark-haired woman, wearing a crinkly black leather dress with a hemline that reached her ankles. Her thin arms hung straight down. She strode purposefully over toward Martel.

"Claude," she said, "I have just seen—"

"Not now, Michelle," Martel said.

"But Claude, I—"

Martel raised up out of his chair. "Not now," he said, his voice hoarse with anger.

She started to protest, changed her mind, swiveled on her heels, and marched out of the room.

"That was my daughter, gentlemen. Do either of you happen to have children?"

He got two nos in response.

"Wise decision."

I got up and took a look at the mass of photographs on the walls. Claude Martel was in most of them. Lionel a few. I didn't see any of Michelle. They were the usual ego-trip pictures, Martel with celebrities and politicians, or studio-posed portraits with words of love and affection—"To My Good Friend Claude Martel"—scrawled on the bottom. Martel certainly stroked his ego with the biggies: He was there shaking hands with, or toasting a drink to, Gerald Ford, Jimmy Carter, Teddy Kennedy, several with Reagan, some when he still had his movie-star good looks. Probably his California-governor days.

The coffeepot was about empty, and Martel had inhaled some five to six inches of his cigar, when the phone finally rang.

Martel watched it patiently and after the sixth ring, picked it up and said, "Hello."

He grunted once or twice, then held the phone out to Roy Whitman. "He wishes to speak to you."

Martel drummed his fingers on the desk and never took his eyes off Whitman.

Whitman took a palm-sized, red-covered spiral notebook from his jacket pocket and began scribbling. "Okay, yes, okay." He raised his eyes to Martel. "He wants me to pick up the merchandise. Doesn't want you involved, sir."

Martel nodded his head. "Tell him okay, but that you will have another man with you." He pointed what was left of his cigar at me. "Mr. Polo."

Whitman relayed the message into the receiver, listened a few seconds, then put his hand over the phone and said, "He doesn't like it. He wants it to be just me."

"Tell him," Martel said, "that I expect to be paying handsomely for the entire package, and that I feel more comfortable with both you and Polo involved."

Whitman passed on the information, went through the routine with his hand over the phone again, and said, "The man says that if there are any police involved, you can kiss the paintings good-bye."

Claude Martel fixed an unwinking stare on Whitman. "You can tell him that there will not be any police involved in this matter. Ever."

♠ ♥ ♣ ♦

"That piece of shit your car?" Whitman asked me.

"It's paid for," I said defensively.

"We'll take mine."

I had to admit there were some seemingly distinctive advantages vis-à-vis Whitman's car. His was a new Lincoln Continental, all gleaming black exterior, with white leather seats. It had flashy-looking mag wheels, and that distinctive little antenna that shows it has a car phone.

"You carrying a gun?" Whitman asked as he opened the car door.

"Can't afford the insurance," I replied. Which was the truth. To work in this business, you need insurance. E&O it's called. Error and omissions. If you make a mistake in your reports, or serve a subpoena on the wrong guy, and he sues, you have to be protected. If by some chance you carry a gun during the course of your employment, as the policy insurance jargon describes it, your premium, already a thousand a year, doubles, at least. And I can't afford that. Still, Mrs. Polo didn't raise a complete idiot, and anytime I'm on a case where there is a lot of money involved, and it's obvious that there are going to be some gentlemen or ladies who will most certainly be carrying something varying from a sharp hatpin to an Uzi submachine gun, I carry a gun. A little .32 revolver was resting snugly alongside my right hip as I slid into Whitman's Lincoln.

The man on the phone, let's call him X because that's what Nero Wolfe always did, and I haven't ever been able to come up with anything as clever, had given Whitman instructions to go to the phone booth in front of the Mission Rock Resort.

"Resort" was a little too fancy a description. The Mission Rock is a restaurant and bar with an outdoor deck overlooking the Bay by Pier 50, on the south Bay waterfront. During the day it gets its share of yuppies and teamsters and longshoremen.

Whitman slipped the key into the car's ignition and turned the motor over. His key ring was made of black metal, one piece about five inches long, tapering to a point on one end. Two smaller, similarly tapered pieces were attached to one side. A Ninja key ring, designed so that when you held it in your fist, you had three sharp objects protruding between your fingers.

Whitman gunned the engine, and the wheels spun as he hit the street. He took a sharp left turn before I had time to fasten my seat belt. I finally got the damn thing buckled as he went through a series of sharp turns and accelerations worthy of a TV detective movie. There are easier ways to identify and then lose a tail, but he seemed to be having fun reliving Steve McQueen's role in *Bullitt*.

He finally slowed down and slipped a cassette into the car's stereo, and we were suddenly surrounded by wailing guitars, and some guy with a gravelly voice singing about a waitress in El Paso.

I never did find out what happened to the waitress because we were mercifully interrupted by Whitman's car phone chirping.

He turned the stereo off and answered the phone with, "Yeah."

A few seconds later he said, "No, baby, I'm working. Can't make it. . . . Uh-huh." Long pause, more "uh-huh"'s, then, "See you later."

"Women," he said to me as he cradled the receiver. "They just won't leave you alone, will they?"

"Sometimes. Usually at the wrong times."

11

The parking lot around the Mission Rock Resort was mostly deserted. There were a few battered old wrecks, two or three campers and VW vans that looked as if they were permanent residents, filled, no doubt, with some of the men and women who might profit from the benefits of the House the Homeless Benefit Ball.

Whitman pulled up right in front of a lone pay telephone. We sat there and listened to the ticking of the car's engine. There was no wind, and it was quiet enough so you could hear the occasional rushing sound of traffic from Third Street, and the nearby freeway. A police or fire engine siren wailed bleakly in the distance.

The phone finally rang, and Whitman got out and slammed the door behind him with more force than was necessary. Maybe it was a rental.

Whitman was scribbling in his notepad as he held the phone between his chin and shoulder.

"Uh-huh" seemed to be one of his favorite phrases.

He hung up and squinted at his notepad. "He says we'll find a package on the bow of a ship, a white twenty-four-foot Bayliner Marine called *The Second Collection*, docked right behind the Mission Rock."

Whitman opened the trunk of his car and took out two flashlights. One was a big, metal five-cell monstrosity, the type uniformed cops use in place of a billy club. The other was a little throwaway plastic job. Guess which one Whitman tossed over to me?

There was a chain-link fence, the gate closed, but not locked, leading to the piers behind the Mission Rock.

Our feet made crunching sounds as we treaded along a gravel path toward the wooden piers. There were three of them, each stretching out to the dark Bay waters.

"You take the one on the right, Pier One," Whitman said. "Remember, the boat's name is *The Second Collection.*"

Great name for a boat, I thought, as I carefully mounted the rotting wooden pier. Must belong either to a loan shark or a priest with a sense of humor.

The planks creaked under my weight as I made my way cautiously down the pier. I played the weak flashlight beam across the bows of the small boats. Some had names painted on the bows, some numbers, some nothing at all. I could see Whitman's flashlight bobbing along slowly on the next pier.

I was almost at the end when I saw it, a smart-looking white cruiser, with blue canvas over the wheelhouse. The lettering was professionally done, neat, precise, black, uppercase, THE SECOND COLLECTION.

"Over here," I yelled toward Whitman.

A small package, no more than two-feet square, was resting on the boat's bow. While the boat's deck was wet from the Bay and the fog, the brown-paper-wrapped package was dry.

I had to lean out to reach for the package. As I touched the bow, the boat moved away a few inches. I stooped to grab the mooring line to pull the boat back, then I heard the rushing footsteps. It was too quick for Whitman to be there. I dropped the line and threw the arm holding the flashlight up in time to block something heavy aiming at my head.

I grunted an obscenity as the pain ran from my forearm up to my shoulder. The flashlight clattered to the decking, sending out a gyrating wave of light. I grabbed for the gun at my hip and had my fingers on the handle when something crashed into my ribs. I rolled away and finally got the gun out of its holster, firing wildly into the blackness.

Someone yelled, "Oh, shit," then I felt another blow in the ribs. I tried rolling away again and succeeded this time. There was a terribly elongated fraction of a second when I was falling free in space, then I hit the water.

I came up spitting and swearing. The Bay water was icy cold. My right hand still held the gun. I pointed it up in the air and fired again. The gun at least was still in working condition. I started to go under again and kicked my way to the top, dog-paddled toward a mooring line, and hung on for dear life.

There was the sound of running feet again, and after a minute or so, a flashlight beam. I tried to keep my teeth from chattering loud enough to be heard, and wrapping my legs around the line, I lined up the front barrel sight on the approaching flashlight beam.

"Freeze," I said as the light got closer. Since I was doing the freezing, it was not exactly an original line.

"Is that you, Polo?" I recognized Whitman's voice. "You okay down there? What the fuck happened?"

I edged my way along the line until I was alongside the dock. "Give me a hand," I told Whitman.

He pulled me up on the dock, and I lay there a minute, spitting out Bay water and shivering.

"Jesus," Whitman said, "you look the shits. What was all the shooting about?"

"Someone jumped me when I was going for the package. I don't know if I hit him."

"I thought you told me you weren't packing a gun?" Whitman protested.

"Good thing I was lying, don't you think?"

I was starting to shiver violently now. Whitman splashed his flashlight beam over me, said, "Jesus," again, then put the light on the bow of *The Second Collection*.

"All's not lost, I guess," he said. "There's a package on the boat."

12

Claude Martel was mad. Well, that really doesn't describe his exact condition. Enraged, furious, irate, incensed, angry, or as someone from the younger generation might say, like real pissed off.

Mostly he was mad because of the story Roy Whitman was telling him.

"You took a shot at this man?" he yelled at me.

"I'd take a shot at anyone who's trying to bash my head in, Mr. Martel."

"Do you have any idea what a risk you took? We may have lost everything."

The fact that I may have lost my life didn't seem to bother him.

He may also have been mad because of the fact that I was walking barefoot over his beautiful carpet, and that I helped myself to a large glass of whisky from a clear bottle with a little silver name tag on it saying scotch, without asking.

My appearance might have had something to do with his general demeanor, also. I was wearing Whitman's leather bomber jacket over an old, stained blanket he had in his car's trunk. My wet and soggy clothes were in a plastic bag

under my arm. The bag had come from a garbage can outside the Mission Rock Resort. You don't want to know what
was in the bag before I emptied it out.

All in all, not a pretty sight. Martel went on cursing
while I replenished my glass. The first drink had gone down
to my stomach like liquid fire, but it ironed out my goose
bumps and helped to stop my shivering. The second drink I
took more time with, rolling the liquor around my mouth,
holding it there a second or two, and letting it trickle down
the throat slowly, as you're supposed to do with fine wines.
The feeling of warmth was almost sensual.

What really got old Martel to blow his stack, though,
was when he unwrapped the package from the bow of *The
Second Collection*. He used a pair of scissors to snip through
the string and undid the paper with the care of a new father
taking off his baby's first diaper. When he saw the painting,
his face went through a quick color change: tan to deep red
to white. I took a quick peek. The painting was a still life of a
bowl of apples lying on a table, done in mostly pastels, in an
impressionist style. Neatly printed across the painting in big
black letters was the word *goniff*.

Martel went through a good minute of cursing in English, French, and what must have been German. My command of foreign languages stops with Italian, but I did know
that *goniff* was a Yiddish word for thief.

Martel pounded a hand on his desk and shouted, "Out,
damn it, out. Both of you. No, Whitman, you stay."

Whitman's lips twisted sardonically as he watched me
turn around. When I was almost to the door, he said, "Hey,
Polo. My jacket."

"Pick it up tomorrow," I said, closing the door behind
me. I wanted to slam it, but it was so heavy and well bal-
anced it just closed with a plopping sound.

Denise Martel was standing by the stairway, an elbow
leaning casually against the handrail. She was wearing an ap-
ricot-colored silk dressing gown with a scoop neck.

"Why, Mr. Polo. You do look a mess. Whatever happened?"

"It's a long story, Mrs. Martel. If you'll . . ."

She walked over and wrapped both her hands around my arm.

"My goodness, we can't let you leave here looking like that. Come with me."

I started to protest, but she increased her pressure on my arm and pulled me toward the stairs.

We went up, past the blue room where I'd met Claude Martel earlier that afternoon. It seemed like weeks ago now. Denise chatted away about how wet I looked, how I mustn't catch a cold, how she'd get me some fresh clothes.

"And a drink. My lord, I bet you could use a drink, couldn't you? First a drink, then a bath."

She opened the door to a large, lavender-and-white bedroom. Nudes, from various artists, in paintings and etchings hung over the bed. The bedcover was white fur of some kind. The bedside nightstand held coffee-table-sized books, featuring the names Degas, Picasso, and Monet. The whole damn house was one big museum.

"Help yourself to a drink, Mr. Polo. I'll be right back."

I wanted to drop my dirty plastic bag, but I was afraid of what it would do to the lavender carpet. A white dresser held an array of liquor bottles and some heavy, cut-crystal glasses. No fancy decanters here, but all top labels. I settled for some Jack Daniel's.

Denise floated back into the room, carrying a long, dark-brown terry-cloth robe. "Here you are, Mr. Polo. Get out of that ridiculous outfit while I start the water."

"Mrs. Martel, I think I . . ."

She shook a finger at me, as if she were scolding a naughty boy. "No, no, you must think of your health. We wouldn't want you catching pneumonia."

I undid the blanket, dropped it on the floor, and put the plastic bag and Whitman's leather jacket on top of it. The robe was one of those "one size fits all" jobs, with a monk's hood. I shivered and took another swig of the Daniel's.

"Poor man, you look so cold," Denise said. "What happened?"

"An accident. I fell in the Bay."

She grabbed my hand and herded me into the bathroom. The bathroom floor was tiled in purple with black grouting. A tub, really a two-person Jacuzzi whirlpool bath, was in the same color as the tile. Water was cascading in sheets out of a gold, thin, flat faucet. It resembled a small waterfall.

"You make yourself comfortable," Denise said. "I'll get some coffee."

The tub wasn't half filled. There was a large stall shower next to it. I turned off the tub water and hopped into the shower, which had more of the purple tile. It took me a few seconds to figure out just how to turn on the damn water. Once I got it working, water began jetting out from three different shower heads. I adjusted the temperature and relaxed. For about a minute.

The glass shower door opened, and Denise Martel climbed in. If you were to describe her body, I guess the best word would be *lush*. She was no kid, and obviously worked at staying in shape, but there was nothing Nautilus or Jane Fonda workout tape about her figure. It looked like the results of massages, visits to diet clinics, a surgical tuck or two, and careful attention to what went past her beautiful lips.

What passed her lips right then was my lips. She pushed me up against the tile and let her tongue work its way into my mouth.

After a minute or two of that, I managed to pull away long enough to say, "What about Claude, won't he . . ."

She started working her mouth down my neck to my shoulder. "Claude understands these things," she said in between nips. "He is a healthy and virile man, but not as healthy and virile as often as he, or I, would like."

She picked up a plastic bottle filled with an emerald-green lotion from a recess in the tile, took off the top, and spilled the lotion on our bodies. She dropped the bottle to the floor and began rubbing the lotion into my skin. Jasmine-scented bubbles and lather started forming as she worked her hands down my chest.

It felt sensational and I tried not to feel guilty. Here I was, with my client's wife, after my client had paid me an enormous amount of money to do a job that he now thought I'd botched. I stopped concentrating on what Denise was doing with her hands long enough to remind myself to call the bank in the morning to see if the check had cleared. Martel was just the kind of guy to stop payment when things didn't go his way.

I fought temptation, just as I was taught to in catechism, but it was a losing fight. The spirit was weak and the flesh was willing. In fact, when Denise dropped to her knees, the flesh was staring her right in the eye. Whoever said good sex had to be dirty had never taken a shower with Denise Martel.

13

I slipped out of bed as quietly as I could. Denise Martel was snoring softly. The lighted digital clock alongside the bed showed it was almost six in the morning. A definite oversleep on my part, but under the circumstances, probably justified.

I got into the monk's robe, wrapped my plastic bag full of clothes and Whitman's jacket in his blanket, and did a barefoot tiptoe out of the room.

I kept on my toes in the hallway and down the stairs and had almost made it to the door, when someone coughed loudly behind me.

"Good morning. Leaving before breakfast?" Michelle Martel said tartly.

She was wearing a powder-blue running outfit and judging from the sweat on her forehead, had just come in from a morning jog.

"Good morning. Yes, I have to run," was the best I could come up with.

"You're Nick Polo, aren't you?"

"Guilty," I replied, reaching for the door handle.

"I'd like to talk to you, Mr. Polo."

"Fine, can we make it later in the day, I'm really in a hurry."

She stood with her hands on her hips, head tilted to one side. "Yes, I can understand why you would be. Let's say your office, at two this afternoon?"

I was in no position to argue. "Yes, let's say that."

I had to drop the blanket on my car's hood and fish through the garbage bag for my keys. When I got home, I left the car in the driveway and hotfooted it up the front steps.

The ever-vigilant Mrs. Damonte fluttered her venetian blinds at me as I passed her front door. The look of disgust on her face was no worse than usual.

I heaved a sigh of relief when I was in my flat, carried my luggage to the kitchen table, and after putting on a pot of coffee, went through the garbage bag. Saving the suit was a possibility, I guess, but the dry cleaner would really have to work at it. The shirt, shorts, and socks went right into the washing machine. I looked at my wallet. The driver's license and private investigator's license were close to mush. Money, thank God, is made of sterner stuff. I laid the bills out on the kitchen sink to dry. The plastic credit cards were indestructible.

The .32 revolver was already starting to turn an ugly brown in spots. I could probably give it a fresh water bath, take it apart, and oil it back to life, but since there was a possibility that someone was walking around wearing a hole from one of the gun's bullets, it seemed safer to find a deep watery grave for the gun.

I carried a cup of coffee into my bedroom, set the radio alarm clock for nine A.M., and flopped down on top of the bed, too sleepy even to discard Martel's robe.

The wailing of a rich alto sax from radio station KJAZ woke me up precisely at nine. Stan Getz? I wondered as I trotted into the bathroom and took another shower. At this rate I'd be sprouting gills in a couple of weeks.

The coffee was overtrained by now, but it still hit the right spots. I scrambled a couple of eggs and toasted an English muffin, then stared at the kitchen wall and tried to figure out just where I stood in all of this confusion.

If I did happen to hit someone with a bullet last night, there was a good chance he'd be in a hospital somewhere, and supposedly, just supposedly, in real life hospitals are supposed to report all gunshot victims to the police.

There was also the possibility that someone reported the sound of gunshots. So, job number one was to check with the police to see if anything was reported.

The first commandment in any investigation is to Cover Thine Own Ass, so I called my old partner, Inspector Paul Paulsen, and explained my needs.

"And Paul, I'd appreciate it if you could pull Jack Cusak's report on the assault at the Martel house the other night."

"If it's on the computer, no problem, Nick. If not, I'll have to go over and dig it out of his files, and someone might ask questions."

"Let's hope it's on the computer then."

Paulsen said he'd call me as soon as he had the information.

Job number two was my trusty, now rusty, gun. The next call went to the San Francisco Police Department Range Master, Chris Sullivan.

"Chris," I said, "I need a small revolver."

"What happened to that .32 I sold you a few months ago?" Sullivan asked.

"What .32?" I said.

There was a fairly long pause. "Shit, Polo, you're an awful lot of trouble. Okay, come on out, I'll fix you up with something."

I was washing up the breakfast dishes when Paulsen called me back.

"No reported gunshot victims, Nick. Quiet night. There was only one incident involving a gun—one guy held up a busload of Japanese tourists."

I groaned inwardly. Paulsen was a great guy, but his

fondness for old, corny jokes was legendary. So, playing the straight man, I said, "Oh, did they catch the guy?"

"No, but we got three hundred pictures of him."

The laughter, one-sided—his side—went on for a minute.

"Good one, Paul. What about Cusak's report?"

"I've got it in front of me. Pretty interesting."

"Read on, Inspector."

Paulsen skimmed quickly through the victim's name, address, and time of incident. "'Victim stated that he was accosted in a room in his family home. Tied to a chair, fingertip amputated. Did not get a look at the suspect. Has no idea why he was attacked.

"'At first victim indicated to the reporting officer that some paintings had been stolen. A subsequent contact by victim showed that he was mistaken. Items he thought were taken were found in another room of the house.'

"Now, here's the interesting stuff, Nick. 'Victim taken to Mt. Zion Hospital. Treated by Dr. Chung for contusions on the scalp and injury to small finger, left hand. The tip of said finger had been amputated and brought to the hospital by the ambulance stewards. Dr. Chung was able to stitch the amputated tip back on the finger. Reporting officer made a follow-up contact with the victim and was told that wounds were self-inflicted when he inadvertently cut himself with a letter opener, then fell to the floor, injuring his head. Victim claimed that when he woke up, he remembered nothing and assumed he had been assaulted.'"

"Thanks, Paul, I owe you one."

"I bribe easy, Nick. But not too easy. Let's make lunch soon."

So the bad guys liked to play real rough. First whack off a little bit of a finger. I wondered if Lionel found the finger-cutting more painful than having to tell that ridiculous story to Cusak.

The Martels, quite a family. The old man apparently

made a fortune on stolen art. He makes sure the cops won't do much in the way of an investigation, because Lionel says nothing was stolen, and his wounds were "self-inflicted."

Lionel says whatever Daddy wants him to say. Denise Martel is a walking, talking sex bomb. I wondered whom else she was fooling around with, and just how much Claude knew about it.

Then there was the daughter, the mannequin-looking Michelle. Claude's daughter, but Denise's? I doubted it. Michelle looked to be in her late twenties, and Denise was a year one way or the other of forty at the most. So Claude had a previous wife. Why not? At his age, and with the money involved, there could have been several ex-wives. I'd find out when Michelle came acalling in the afternoon.

Lembi had hinted that Claude Martel was in financial trouble, which was why he thought Martel was peddling the Chagall, Vandyke, and Renoir in Europe. I'd have to find out about that from my two best confidential sources.

Now when you think of a private investigator's confidential sources, you come up with people like cops with access to restricted files, a clerk at the Department of Motor Vehicles, cabdrivers, hotel doormen, bartenders, newspaper reporters. Ah, those were the old days, my friends. My two main sources are the people at IBM and Hewlett-Packard.

I walked down to my office and turned on the Big Blue computer and the HP printer. The black screen came to life, and printed yellow lines began asking me simple questions, like, date and time. When these were answered correctly, I punched in the magic four letters—SCOM—and the screen gurgled for a second, then put up what they like to call in computer land a menu, with a list of twenty data-base companies that can supply you with all sorts of juicy information.

I selected the one that handled state assessor records, fed in the name Claude Martel, and watched the typed data roll down the screen faster than I could read it. The HP printer silently documented it for me as fast as it came up on the computer. Three pages' worth. When the screen was finished with Claude, I put in the name Lionel Martel. No property under this name was the only information they had for Lionel.

I studied the printouts. Martel had property all over the state, listed under Claude Martel, Inc. From San Diego to Sacramento, with plenty of stops in between, the major pieces right in the Bay Area. Mostly large buildings, some designated as shopping centers. Under the heading "last transaction," the word *refi-* for refinance popped up quite often.

Lembi said that Martel had holdings all over the world. Unfortunately, my computer wizard menu had nothing to cover that. I knew someone who did.

He was expensive, but I had Martel's five thousand dollars to play with. Or did I? I made a quick call to the bank and found out the check had cleared, so I called a man in Southern California.

You don't get any printed material from this chap, nothing in the mail, nothing faxed to you, nothing with his name on it. Everything is done over the phone. He's competent, resourceful, and reliable, and a former federal bank examiner, but the way he obtains his material is illegal. He's a master hacker and uses his computer to get into places mine has never heard of, so he's expensive, and also hard to deal with. But worth the struggle.

I gave him Martel's name and the rumor that he was in financial difficulties. "I'd like as much detail on this as possible," I said.

"I'd like five hundred bucks," he responded.

"The minute I get the info, you get the money, my friend."

"We're not friends, Polo, we're associates, and you'll have it by tomorrow morning."

Like I said, hard to deal with. My afternoon looked as if it was going to be busy, which left me with the rest of the morning, and nothing better to do than that old standby, return to the scene of the crime.

14

I made a quick stop at the police range. Sullivan had a little S&W .32, identical to the one that had taken a Bay bath, waiting for me.

Ever the professional, he insisted that I shoot the thing before relinquishing possession. The gun, with a snub-nose barrel, worked fine; it had little accuracy over a few feet, but I wasn't getting it for target shooting. Not a hell of a lot of stopping power either, but if you hit someone with it, there would be some damage done. It barely kicked when you pulled the trigger, and it made a sufficiently loud noise when fired, and best of all, it was light and easily concealed.

When Sullivan was satisfied that the gun worked, and that it looked as if I wouldn't shoot my foot off with it, he accepted a suitable amount of cash and bid me good hunting.

The parking lot at the Mission Rock Resort was jammed. I parked in front of a fire hydrant and went inside. A good lunch crowd was in full swing. There is an upper patio deck with a bar, and a lower deck with a bar. The lower patio's food ran to hot dogs and hamburgers, the upper got a little fancier. I bought a cup of coffee in a Styrofoam cup and wandered out to the piers.

A heavy breeze was stippling the surface of the Bay with

whitecaps. Two huge, gray Navy ships and an Exxon tanker with a rusty hull were in drydock in the nearby shipyard.

It had been too dark to notice last night, but faded white paint on the decking showed the pier numbers. I went back down Pier One.

The Second Collection was still in its mooring. I stooped to check the deck. There were spots of what looked like dried blood, but human blood or fish blood was beyond my humble investigative skills.

I didn't see any bullet holes in the deck, or nearby boats, but from the angle I was firing, the bullet should have been going in an upper trajectory, and it either hit the guy who attacked me or took a harmless little flight over the top of the restaurant.

A young kid wearing paint-spattered white pants, a gray sweatshirt, and a battered Giants baseball cap was doing a varnish job on the deck of one of the boats.

"Can I help you, mister?" he asked.

"Yes. *The Second Collection*. Is the owner around?"

The kid tipped his cap back and smiled. "He's around Tahiti somewhere, on vacation. You interested in the boat?"

"Is she for sale?"

"Sale or rent, mister. I'm looking after it."

"Someone told me about it. I can't think of his name, met him in a bar, said he rented it a few days ago."

This time the hat came off and he scratched a thatch of blond hair. "Not that boat, mister. It's been tied up for two weeks now. Hasn't moved from the dock. Who was this guy?"

"Just a guy I met at a bar. I guess he gave me the wrong info."

I sat in the restaurant and had a hamburger and beer and enjoyed the view. It looked as if someone had just picked *The Second Collection* as the drop point at random. Why that boat? Why the Mission Rock? Why not?

I walked out to my car, opened the trunk, and palmed

the .32 I had used last night. I walked back to the piers, this time taking number two, the one that Whitman had wandered down last night, walked to the end, saw that no one was paying any particular attention to me, and bent down and dropped the gun over the side.

When I got back to my flat, I checked the mail: two bills, rather large, two checks, rather small. My answering machine showed two calls. I ran the tape back and played them. Both from Roy Whitman; the first fairly civilized: "Call me as soon as possible, please." The second a little less civilized: "Call me right away. And I want my coat." I had forgotten about his leather bomber jacket.

Michelle Martel arrived right at two o'clock. She had the air of someone who always arrived on time and expected others to do the same.

She was dressed in a gray, double-breasted jacket, with matching skirt and a white blouse. Her lipstick and mascara had been applied with a lot of care. She looked like a high-priced model on the way to a photo assignment. All business.

I took her into the front room. She gave it a hard look. "This is your office?"

"This is as close as it gets, Miss Martel. What can I do for you?"

"Why did you fuck Denise last night?"

I did say she looked all business, didn't I? "What makes you think I did, and why do you ask?"

She dropped her handbag to the floor and perched on the edge of my leather sofa, a hand over each knee.

"Denise is always fucking someone or other. I don't know why Claude puts up with her," she said.

It always made me cringe when someone called their parents by their first names. If I had called my father John, just once, he'd have put on his heaviest work shoes and painted a bull's-eye on the seat of my pants.

"I take it Denise is not your natural mother."

"Certainly not. My mother died when I was born. Claude has been married four times. I'm amazed Denise has lasted so long. Claude must be getting senile. Fucking, that's all she's around for. She fucks when Claude wants, and whom he wants."

"But Lionel is your brother?"

"Half brother, Mr. Polo. Claude has said that the smartest thing he's done since my birth is have a vasectomy."

"How do you and Lionel get along?"

"All right now. We had a difficult childhood. He wanted to play doctor with me all the time. Poor boy isn't very bright. He's upset because he knows Claude will never turn the business over to him. I'm quite capable of handling it, but Claude's a frontline chauvinist. He thinks a woman's place is in bed, with her legs in the air. I had to beg him to let me take over the galleries. We'd both like to know Claude's plans. He's not getting any younger. Do you speak French, Mr. Polo?"

"I never got passed 'Chevrolet Coupe.'"

"Claude has a favorite saying: 'Après moi la fin du monde.' After I die, it's the end of the world. We'd all like to know just what he has put in his will."

A reluctant smile came to her stern face. "Denise is quite beautiful, isn't she?"

"Quite. But you didn't come here to talk about Denise Martel's looks."

"No, I did not. I would like to know just what you and that other gentleman are doing for Claude."

"By 'other gentleman' I take it you mean Roy Whitman?"

"That's right. Claude is upset, very upset, and I want to know what is going on. Could I have something to drink, please?"

"Sure, coffee, tea, a glass—"

"A martini. Vodka. Russian if you have it."

I keep my vodka in the freezer. The label had a Russian

name, Popov, but it was made in nearby Menlo Park, not Moscow. I like to do what little I can for the trade deficit. I poured it over some ice, added a twist of lemon and a drop of vermouth, and carried it back to the front room.

Michelle had taken off her jacket and her shoes. She was sprawled on the couch, showing a lot of leg.

"Thank you," she said, accepting the drink.

"You're welcome, Miss Martel. Now maybe you can—"

"What are you doing for Claude?"

"You better ask him."

Her head bobbed down to her drink, like a bird's, taking a little sip, then tilting her head back to swallow. She didn't look as if she handled martinis on a regular basis.

"I could hear Claude last night. He didn't sound very happy with you, Mr. Polo. Are you still working for him?"

"I don't really know."

"I really don't think so," she said. "He was yelling about you, saying you had fucked things up badly."

She paused, waiting for a reaction. I didn't give her one.

"Since you are no longer working for Claude, I'd like you to work for me."

"Doing exactly what?"

"I'd like to know just what you were doing for Claude, and exactly what happened to Lionel."

"Why don't you ask Lionel?" I said.

"He's absolutely terrified of Claude. He won't tell me a thing."

"Were you there the night Lionel was hurt?"

"In Carmel. On gallery business."

Carmel is a couple of hours' drive down the coast.

"As far as I know, I'm still working for your father, Miss Martel, and I'm sure he wouldn't want me talking to you without his permission."

She took another sip of her drink, set it down on the arm of the couch, stood up, smoothed down her skirt, and walked over to me. She put both arms around my neck and pulled my head down close to hers.

"I don't think he would approve of your fucking Denise without his permission either."

Her arms were strong and pulled me closer. She kissed hard, her teeth mashing against my lips, causing me to wince and move back.

She let go of my neck. "You'd rather fuck a fat cow like Denise, wouldn't you?" she said, anger flushing her cheeks. She picked up her purse and wiggled her feet into her shoes.

She turned back when she got to the door. "When Claude tells you that you are no longer working for him, call me."

I went to the front window and saw her get into a white Mercedes coupe. I took the remains of her martini to the kitchen and dumped it down the sink. Denise and Michelle Martel. Different as night and day. Different as soft and hard. Different as tax increases and revenue enhancements. And both of them after my pink, shell-like body. What is it you have, Polo? I asked myself. Charm, wit, good looks, a diversified stock portfolio? In the immortal words of Mrs. Damonte, "nopa." What I had was some information on Claude and Lionel Martel's problems, and both Denise and Michelle wanted to know just what was going on.

It was time to see Lionel Martel. If he made a heavy pass at me, I'd turn everything I had over to the man from Interpol and go to Vegas for a couple of days.

15

I was almost out the door when I remembered Whitman's jacket. It was where I'd left it, on top of the dryer. Being nosy by birth and inquisitive by profession, I went through the pockets. Two cheap ballpoint pens, a few crumpled old Kleenex, and the red-jacketed spiral notebook he was scribbling in last night. I opened the book up. The first page had boldly printed words—*alone, no Martel, no cops*—and the second page had the words *Second Collection* and *Pier 1*.

That was it. The rest were just lined blank pages. Pier 1. The son of a bitch. He had sent me down Pier 1, knowing what was waiting, while he trooped merrily down his way on the other pier. Or had he come back around and knocked me out himself? No, I had seen his flashlight beam on the other pier.

Good old Roy Whitman. The son of a bitch. I know I was being repetitive, but at least I was accurate.

The pickup at Mission Rock was a setup. I wasn't supposed to be part of the package. When Claude Martel had insisted that I go along, they had to pick a nice, quiet, dark spot. That call to Whitman in his car must have been his partner in crime, telling Whitman everything was arranged.

I called the number Whitman had left on my answering machine and got connected to his answering machine. Familiar music came on first, then Whitman's voice. "This is Roy Whitman. Leave a message and I'll get back to you." I hung up, scratching my chin, trying to place the music, then it came to me. It was the theme from the *Rockford Files*. It reaffirmed my opinion of Whitman. He was a dumb, corny son of a bitch.

I thumbed through the yellow pages and found his ad, profile and all. Whitman's office was on Ringold Street.

Ringold was a little alleyway in the South of Market area of the city, now called SOMA. The small, blue-collar businesses that once dominated that area of town were being driven out by business taxes and increasing rents. As they moved out, flashy discos, gay bars, leather joints, and upscale restaurants began taking over.

I panicked when I turned up Ninth Street looking for a parking space. There were four black-and-white police cars and a solo bike parked near the entrance to Ringold. I had thoughts of Roy Whitman's body polka-dotted with bullet holes, until I saw the reason for the big police turnout. There was a Law Enforcement Uniform shop on the corner of Ninth and Ringold. Lord knows I want the boys and girls in blue to look as spiffy as possible, but do they have to grab all the illegal parking spots? Can't they just double-park like truck drivers do? I had to drive a full block away to find a vacant yellow zone.

Whitman's place was an old wood clapboard affair that had been remodeled recently. There was an iron gate blocking entrance to the front steps. There were two doorbells, one marked MORRIS ELECTRIC, the other WHITMAN INVESTIGATIONS. I rang Whitman's doorbell several times and waited. Nothing. I tried the Morris bell and got the same results. Mounted on the wall, about eight feet inside the gate, was a small piece of metal in a half-moon shape. Behind that there would be a button to release the front gate, so that someone leaving could buzz their way out. So close and yet so far.

The garage door was solid, except for a weathered brass mailbox slot. I peeked through, but couldn't see anything.

It was too light to try anything fancy, especially with all those police cars close by, so I went back to the car.

Lionel Martel's residence was located on Pine Street, just a few feet from the city's financial district, and within walking distance of the Embarcadero. I parked in the passenger unloading zone in front of the building. I tilted my head back and looked up; I stopped counting when I got past thirty floors.

The front entrance was all marble, light brown with green trim. The lobby was more marble, with brass accents everywhere: handrails, flowerpots, light fixtures, elevator doors. Even Mrs. Damonte would have worn herself out polishing all that brass.

A eager-looking young man in a beige security uniform, trimmed in green, was standing behind a brass-fronted counter. "Can I help you, sir?" he asked me.

"How would I get to Mr. Lionel Martel's apartment?"

The paunch below his belt disappeared then rose to inflate his chest. "Mr. Martel? He's in the penthouse, sir. I'll have to ring before I let you in."

He picked up a phone and began punching buttons on a console that would have done justice to the spaceship *Enterprise*, smiling at me all the while.

"Mr. Martel, there's a gentleman in the lobby to see you, sir." He raised his eyebrows to me. "Mr. . . . ?"

I gave him my name.

"Mr. Nick Polo, sir."

His smile began melting, and his head nodded. "Yes, sir. I understand. I'll—"

"Tell him his father sent me," I told the now-frowning kid.

For some reason this seemed to make him happy. The smile appeared again as he relayed the message.

"Just one second, Mr. Martel."

He handed me the receiver.

"Lionel," I said. "We met at the poker game the other night. I'm doing a job for your father. We have to talk."

"Uh, yes, I understand, but you've caught me at an awkward time, Mr. Polo, perhaps we could—"

I said, "Under the circumstances we don't have much time to waste."

"Yes, yes. Just a moment, please." I heard the phone clatter. He was back on the line in less than a minute. "Give me fifteen minutes, Mr. Polo. I've got to shower. Fifteen minutes, all right?"

"Fine." I handed the phone back to the guard. "He wants me to go up in a few minutes."

"Right, sir." He pointed to a bank of elevators behind him. "Those will take you to the residential units, sir." He gave me a brief rundown on the building. There were five banks of elevators. Three on the opposite end of the building that went up to the twentieth floor. "Those are for the commercial tenants, sir. The two banks behind me are for the residents."

I wasn't paying much attention to him. I was thinking about Lionel Martel. He sounded nervous as hell. Why? No one gets that nervous over a shower. So he had a visitor, and he wanted him or her out before I got there. No problem. Can't blame the lad for that.

"How about parking, that a problem here?" I asked my tour guide.

"No, sir. Three floors of underground parking. All of the residential tenants are allotted two spaces. Commercial tenants can lease as many as they want, and it's open to public parking."

"How do I get to the parking lot?"

He pointed toward the far end of the building. "Any of the elevators, sir. Or the stairway, of course."

I thanked him and hotfooted it down to the other end of the building, found the stairway, and climbed down.

The garage was like all garages, smelling of raw concrete and gasoline. Since there were three floors of parked cars, and since if Martel did have a visitor, there was no way of my knowing just what floor he or she parked on, I waited by the exit gate where a man in a uniform identical to my friend's in the lobby was receiving exorbitant fees from the poor souls of the world who had to pay for their parking.

Patience has its rewards. About ten minutes later a British racing-green Jaguar sedan, with my old poker buddy Chuck at the wheel, stopped for the parking attendant, handed the man a bill, and waited with outstretched hand for his change.

When I got back upstairs, my friend at the reception desk spotted me and called Martel again.

"He says to go right up, Mr. Polo."

♠ ♥ ♣ ♦

Martel greeted me at the door. He was wearing starched khaki pants and a blue button-down shirt. A black silk sling was draped over his neck, supporting his heavily bandaged left hand.

"Thanks for waiting," he said, closing the door after us.

Living in San Francisco as long as I have, you get used to the views, but I have to admit I was a little stunned by what Lionel Martel had to look at when there was nothing on TV.

The outside walls were glass, floor to ceiling. The views were like paintings, the windows acted as frames, looking out on the whole panorama of the Bay, from the Golden Gate Bridge over to the East Bay. Though we were some blocks from the water, the height made it appear as if you could jump out and land in the Bay. Something I knew from personal experience wasn't worth the trip.

I guess Martel was used to seeing people gape.

"Nice, isn't it?" he said casually.

"Very."

"Can I get you something to drink?" he asked.

"No, thanks. It must be tough," I said, pointing to his hand. "Showering with that thing."

"Yes, yes, a damn nuisance."

The penthouse was a lot more modern than the Martel residence. The flooring was terra-cotta tiles in a grid pattern, brown, with white caulking. The walls were all white. A large oil painting, at least four by six feet, was set in a brass frame over the couch. The painting was just smears of thick white paint and looked as if it was made of the same stucco material as on the wall behind.

The chairs were in a brown that almost matched the couch.

"Sit down, please, Mr. Polo. I seem to remember that I owe you some money from that poker game."

"Yes. Eight hundred dollars. No hurry on that though. What I want to talk to you about is what happened after the game."

Lionel took in a deep breath. "I told the police everything, and—"

"Bullshit, Lionel. I'm working for your father, remember. I've seen the police reports. The cops don't buy the fairy tale about your cutting yourself and passing out. Neat trick, a guy cutting off his finger, then knocking himself on the back of the head. But since you changed your story, said there was no theft, and everything was an accident, they'll drop it. The police don't go looking for problems. It's not like they don't have enough work already."

"Yes, I'm sorry, I just—"

"You know what happened last night, don't you? About the painting we recovered?"

"Yes. I know. It's just that, have you spoken to father today?"

"Yes." Technically anyway. It was in the A.M. when he

kicked me out of his office. "And your sister. And your mother. Or stepmother I guess it is. Nice lady, isn't she?"

"Yes, yes." He slumped into the chair across from me. "What do you want to know?"

"What happened after you left the card game?"

"The waiter told me there was a call from father. I thought it might be important. I went to father's office. Once I was inside the door, someone hit me from behind." His good hand went to the back of his head and began massaging it. "When I came to, I was tied down in father's chair. A man, he had a ski mask, one of those full-face things, over his head. He—"

"What about his clothes?" I asked. "Was he wearing a tuxedo?"

Lionel Martel gave an abrupt nod. "Yes, I think so. He told me to give him the combination for the vault. I refused, of course. Then he put a gag in my mouth. Would you care for a drink?"

"Sure, why not?"

He got to his feet and walked over to a red and black lacquered Venetian commode, opened the door, and pulled out a bottle of Glenlivet. He was fumbling the job with one hand, so I got up to help.

"Let me," I said, taking the bottle from his hand, digging two Waterford glasses out of the commode, and pouring us both two heavy slugs of the scotch.

He accepted his glass and took a big swig. Too big. He started coughing and some of the liquor spilled from his lips. He put his glass down and wiped his mouth with his sleeve.

"Just talking about it gets me jumpy," he said, picking his glass up again.

"I believe it, Lionel. Take your time. You were saying he put a gag in your mouth."

"Yes. Exactly. He hit me a couple of times, in the stomach, then took the gag out again. I still refused to give him the combination, so he put the gag back in my mouth and took out a knife. He threatened to cut off my finger. I couldn't believe he'd actually do it, but he did. It . . . it happened so fast. I couldn't believe it. He threatened to cut me again, more than my finger this time. There was nothing else I could do. I had to give him the combination."

"Lionel, you held out a lot longer than I could have. I would have had the vault door opened and asked how he wanted the paintings wrapped as soon as he pulled out that knife."

"Really?" he said, as if he was hoping to believe me. "Father thinks that—well, he was upset about the loss, naturally."

"Naturally. But there was nothing else you could have done. From my conversations with your father, he seems quite proud of the way you handled yourself."

That got me another "Really?"

"After the vault was opened, what happened?"

"He hit me again, I passed out, and when I woke up, there was blood everywhere, and my—my fingertip was lying on the floor beside me. I got sick, violently sick. Then the security man, Whitman, came in and found me. He untied me and I told him to get help." For the first time a bit of spark came into Lionel Martel's eyes. "I made sure that the vault door was closed before the police got there. I made sure of that, at least."

"Why did you hire Whitman?"

His eyes dropped to the floor. "Whitman had helped me in a small matter. He was very efficient. I had used him before, so I knew he could be trusted."

"The man who attacked you. Do you think it could have been the waiter, the one who told you about the phone call?"

"I don't really know. I guess so. After he told me about the call, I was stopped by a couple of people on the dance floor. Not for long, just to say 'Hi, how are you,' that kind of thing. I don't recall the waiter following me, but he would have had plenty of time to get to father's office before I did."

"I saw Chuck, one of our poker-playing companions, in the garage."

The fingers on his unbandaged hand turned restless. He kept tapping them on the rim of his glass, like a man who'd recently given up smoking. "Oh, you mean Mr. Bodine. Yes, he's a good family friend. Is there anything else, Mr. Polo?"

"No, that's about it," I said, though I would have loved for him to tell just what dirty little secret Roy Whitman had helped him with.

I used the public phone in the building's lobby to check for messages on my answering machine. There was one call, from Gene Lembi, the Interpol guy: "Mr. Polo, please meet me this evening at six, at the Meridien Hotel. I'll be at the bar in the Justin Brasserie. Please come. I have something that I'm sure will interest you."

Clever fellow with words, Mr. Lembi. How can you resist when someone says they have "something I'm sure will interest you"?

It was almost five-thirty, and the Meridien was just a few blocks away. I checked under Sporting Goods in the phone directory and found a shop specializing in golf equipment just a block from the Meridien. I might as well do a little shopping for burglary tools while waiting to see Lembi.

The Meridien is one of the city's newer hotels, the outside an ugly jacket of beige marble, the inside lobby more cold marble and employees with warm smiles.

Lembi was waiting at the bar. He was wearing another beautifully tailored suit, this one a solid dark blue. He greeted me with that French touch, handshakes, and pats on the back.

"What can I get you to drink?" he asked.

"Vodka Gibson up," I said. I had been to the hotel bar before. They make a great Gibson. They should, since the price of one drink just about equaled the amount I had paid for the liter of vodka in my freezer.

Lembi ordered my drink, and a Picon for himself. He poured out small talk, about the weather and the difference between the franc and the dollar, while we waited for the drinks to arrive.

After I had taken my first sip, he took a small package from the chair beside him. "Yours, I think, Mr. Polo."

It was a plain brown bag. Inside was a .32 revolver.

"I took the liberty of cleaning it up," Lembi said. "I think it will still be of service."

I went back to my drink to stall for time. I was impressed. If that was the gun I had thrown off the dock, and I'd have to get home and check the serial number to be sure, then Lembi had gone through a lot of trouble to retrieve it. He must have watched me drop it into the Bay. He'd have to get to it before the tides got to it. Even then, finding it could be a problem. The San Francisco Bay bears no resemblance to clear, blue Caribbean waters. Visibility was measured in fractions of inches. Even with a powerful underwater light, Jacqueline Bisset could swim by your nose in a see-through T-shirt and you'd never enjoy the view. A metal detector would help, but it would be confused by the years of beer cans, old anchors, motor parts, and God knows what that finds its way to the black mud bottom of the Bay.

"You shouldn't have gone to all that trouble," was what I finally said.

Lembi shrugged. "A man in your line of work certainly needs a gun. In fact, I'm sure you need all the protection you can get."

I may have been critical of the way Whitman checked for a tail last night, but it was certainly better than what I had done, not check at all.

"I'm still working for Claude Martel."

His smile was a rapid flash. "I know. I don't want to come between you and your employer." He took a swallow of his Picon. "I would want you to feel free to come to me if you get into a situation that is, shall we say, difficult. That may bring you in conflict with the local police."

"You mean if I find out that Claude Martel is dealing in hot paintings, I tell you and you'll keep me out of it."

He affirmed the conclusion with a nod, a pleased grin splitting his face. "Exactly." He gestured to the brown bag. "No one knows about the gun except the two of us. I'm curious about why you got rid of it. Obviously you used it recently. Where, I don't know. Why you picked that spot to dispose of it puzzles me. There are much better places available, where the water is deeper."

I finished my drink and stood up. "From now on, if I find you, or anyone else trailing me, I'll tell Martel about your interest in him."

"That would not be wise, Mr. Polo. I was hoping we could work together on this."

"Maybe we can. We're both *un peu louche*."

♠ ♥ ♣ ♦

I used the lobby phone. There was a call from Claude Martel on my answering machine.

I dialed Martel's house. The butler answered the phone.

"Mr. Martel, please. Nick Polo calling."

"My son says you went to see him today," Claude Martel said when he was on the line.

"As far as I know, I'm still working for you. I needed some information."

"I was not happy with the way you handled things last night," he said.

"I gathered that."

"I may have been too harsh. These people are barbarians. Did you see what they did to my painting? It will take a lot of work, and luck, to restore it. There has been no further contact. Do you think you could have killed the man who attacked you?"

"It's possible, but I doubt it. I checked. No one has reported any bullet wounds at any of the city hospitals. No reports of any shootings last night either."

"Then why the delay?" he demanded.

"Maybe they're just testing your patience."

He snorted. "I doubt that. You have heard nothing from your underworld sources?"

"Not a word."

"Do you have any suggestions?"

"I'd like to try and run down that waiter. The one who gave the message to Lionel."

"I had Whitman check with the caterer. They claim they hired no one matching that description."

I believed them. He never would have passed the hygiene test with those ditchdigger's fingernails. But the two greatest burglary tools in the world are a pair of coveralls or a tuxedo. Coveralls and a toolbox will get you into most buildings. One guy had made a clean sweep of a half dozen businesses simply by walking into stores with the name of a cash register company stitched on his back. He'd wait until the owner was out, someone else was running the place, and he'd pick up the working cash register for repairs, with the cash still in it. A tuxedo would have worked just as well at the Martel house. Who counts how many waiters come in the servants' entrance?

"I've been trying to get in touch with Whitman," I said to Martel.

"Don't bother. He's here at the house with me. He'll be staying here until the thieves contact us again. Look for the waiter. But be careful. I don't want these people arrested, I just want my paintings. Whitman will handle the transfers from now on. I don't want you spooking these people, is that understood?"

"I don't trust Whitman," I told him.

"I agree. That's one of the reasons I've got him here with me. I want you here, too. Come as soon as you can."

"It'll be an hour or so."

"All right. Keep checking with your answering machine for messages. Understand?"

He must have assumed I understood because he hung up without waiting for an answer.

17

I checked my rearview mirror for several blocks and couldn't see anyone following me. That didn't mean they weren't there of course. If an agency like Interpol wanted you followed, they would have the money and the manpower to do the job properly. Three or four sets of cars, radio hookups, the works.

I crisscrossed around town, doubled back a couple of times, keeping a very slow pace, forcing the cars behind me to pull around if they wanted to keep up a normal rate of speed. No one seemed to be hanging back. Then I got on the Bayshore Freeway and after cutting across two lanes of traffic, bringing out a chorus of honking horns and middle fingers sticking in the air, pulled over to the side of the road with the car's hazard lights blinking. I waited a couple of minutes, then took off. If anyone was still on my tail now, they deserved to be.

I got off the freeway and headed back downtown. I parked on Ninth Street and got the package from the sporting goods store from the car's backseat. I unwrapped the golf gloves. Golfers only use one glove, but I needed both, one left hand, one right hand. All the best burglars wear them now; thin leather that fits like a second skin. A little more expensive than the white cotton funeral gloves that the bad guys used to favor, but well worth the price. The only other item in the bag was a golf-ball retriever, a thin aluminum rod not more than three feet long to begin with, but which telescoped out a full twelve feet. There was a little cup at the end, made up of five pieces of curved aluminum, finger shaped. The idea is that when a golfer puts his ball in a lake or creek, he extends the pole out and scoops it out of the water. I bent all but one of the metal fingers back, took my Swiss Army knife out of the glove compartment, got out of the car, and walked over to Whitman's place.

I pushed the doorbell a few times, got no response, so I went to work. The front lock would no doubt have been pickable, but it would have taken some time, and unlike those experts in the movies who can pop a lock in seconds, it sometimes takes me long, nervous minutes to get the job done. The retriever made quick work of it. I angled it through the metal grillwork, kept pushing out more of the rod until it reached the remote opener, then wiggled the end of the gadget until it made contact with the button, and the door buzzed open.

I took the steps two at a time. A plastic MORRIS ELEC-TRIC sign was attached to the first door. The other had Whit-man's name stenciled on it. It also had two locks on it. The first was no problem, a Schlage wafer lock. The other was a different thing entirely, a heavy brass tumbler baby.

I took out my Army knife, removed the tweezers, and opened the fish-scale blade. The blade had been altered for me by a professional burglar. I used the tweezers as a shim and raked the lock with the blade. In under a minute I'd located the master wafer and the lock clicked open. Feeling rather proud of myself, I attacked the tumbler lock.

Five minutes later I felt anything but proud; just nervous, sweaty, and frustrated. I'd need something a little fancier to crack the damn thing.

I packed away my tools, went back to the car, and drove

home, leaving the car at the curb, went into the basement, and from a toolbox took out a "lockgun." If this didn't pop Whitman's door, I'd have to forget it. Of course all of this meant more rearview mirror watching, and stopping on the freeway again. I was in anything but a cheerful mood when I got back to Whitman's.

I had left the front gate unlatched, and it was still in that condition when I got back to the building.

Just to be safe, I pushed the doorbell again, then ran up the stairs. The lockgun looks like a cheap space gun kids bought years ago; red metal, with a long, exposed trigger. A small steel tension wrench was taped to the handle. I slid the wrench into Whitman's tumbler lock, inserted the pick at the end of the gun alongside it, and began pulling the trigger as fast as I could, wiggling the wrench at the same time. In theory, the pick, powered by the trigger action, strikes all the cylinder bottom pins simultaneously, and pushing on the tension wrench, the plug turns to the open position, and bingo, you're in. That's exactly what happened, in less than thirty seconds.

I opened the door a few feet, felt for the light switch, turned it on, took a quick glance, then turned on my heels and got out of there fast in case Whitman had invested in a silent burglar alarm.

I left the front gate open again, walked hurriedly down the block, found a sewer grate, and dropped the lockgun down it. Hated to do that. A real handy gadget. Supposedly made for locksmiths only, but available to anyone with access to hardware catalogs. They cost about fifty bucks. Not cheap. But unless you're an authorized locksmith, they are rightly considered burglary tools and can cost you a lot of time in jail.

I crossed Ninth Street to my car, threw the golf-ball retriever in the trunk, got in behind the wheel, turned the motor on, and drove up half a block and waited. Twenty minutes and no sign of a burglar alarm company truck or the cops.

I decided to wait another ten minutes to be safe, then wandered back to Whitman's office.

It wasn't much. Two rooms. All black metal office furniture, a desk, filing cabinets, and a table. There was a Canon copy machine, a fax machine, and an IBM Selectric typewriter. No computer. Backward devil. An old-fashioned iron safe squatted alongside the desk.

There was a cork bulletin board on one wall. His state license was pinned there, along with a schedule for the San Francisco Police Department's golf club. Maybe I should leave Whitman the ball-scooper.

Another wall had a business calendar from an automotive supply store with a busty redhead in a bathing suit the required two sizes too small. She was holding a crescent wrench as if it were the flower bouquet they give to Miss America.

The desk drawer was locked, but it was no match for my trusty Swiss Army knife. Nothing in the center drawer but paper clips, a business-card holder, pencils, and a year-old calendar. The other drawers were about as interesting, except for an old Luger automatic in a well-oiled holster.

Whitman had a business calendar on top of the desk. I thumbed through it for the past few weeks. What looked like Lionel Martel's name popped up a week ago. The scribbling was so bad I couldn't make much else out.

I went to the file cabinets. There were two of them, four drawers high. I found the M's. Nothing under the name Martel. I went back poking around the office. The table holding the copy and fax machines had a single drawer. The drawer held manuals for the copy and fax machines. Nothing else.

I sighed and went over to the old safe. It stood over three feet high, on short, stubby, iron-claw legs. It looked solid and dependable, and I wondered just where it had spent its early life, and whose money, gold, or jewels it had protected. The front was decorated in faded gold leaf. The combination dial was pitted and chipped. I gave the handle a pull, hoping that the safe was nothing more than Whitman's idea of office decoration. No such luck. The door was locked. I gave the combination a twirl and heard the precise clicking of the tumblers. There was no easy way into that old beauty. No sandpapering the fingers and feeling the tumblers fall into place. Without a combination you would have to blow it, or have some professional peeling tools.

What did Whitman have that was so important it had to be locked up in this old beauty? His checkbook, accounts receivable, employee records, telephone bills? The Martel file? All items I would have loved to have gotten a look at. The safe was big enough to hold a half dozen paintings of the size we found on the bow of *The Second Collection.*

So all my hard work and second-story skills had really provided nothing in the way of information. Except that Whitman was a careful man. Something I already knew.

I sat behind his desk and started thumbing through the addresses on his Rolodex. Lionel Martel had a card, with his apartment address. There were listings for attorneys, insurance companies, just names with telephone numbers and no addresses. I had started looking under the letter *M* for Martel and was all the way through the *A*'s when I found something interesting under the *B*'s. Charles Bodine. The Martel family friend, and my old poker friend. What the hell was Whitman doing with Bodine's addresses and phone numbers? The card showed both a San Francisco and a Houston address, with corresponding phone numbers. I found a blank card on the Rolodex, took it over to Whitman's typewriter, and typed out a duplicate.

18

Claude Martel was waiting for me in his office. He looked a lot older than he had at our last meeting. He was sitting in his chair, but his back wasn't as straight, the shoulders were more stooped, and the lines on his face looked deeper. He had one of his monster cigars going.

He raised a questioning eyebrow at the package under my arm.

"Whitman's coat," I said. "He lent it to me last night, after my little dip in the Bay."

"What about Whitman?" Martel asked. "What have you got on him?"

I took the notepad from Whitman's leather jacket and handed it to Martel. "When Whitman answered the phone at Mission Rock Resort, he wrote down the pier number. Number one. There are three piers there. When we went to get the painting, he specifically sent me down to Pier One. He knew what was there, or rather, who was there."

Martel studied the notepad. "This is not conclusive. Maybe he didn't know which pier was which. You're wasting your time with Whitman. If he is involved, why doesn't he just ask for the money? He knows I'll pay it."

"Whitman's not the main man in this, Mr. Martel. He

wouldn't have the brains to handle it. It's someone who knows you and knows how you operate."

He stared at the burning tip of his cigar for a long time, then looked at me as if trying to remember who I was and what I was doing there.

"I've thought of that, of course, Mr. Polo."

"Did anyone but you and Lionel have the combination to the safe?"

"No," he said harshly. "And Lionel didn't have it until recently, when I found it necessary to give it to him."

We were interrupted by a knock on the door. Denise Martel stuck her pretty head into the room and announced, "Dinner is being served, darling."

"Out," Martel shouted. "We'll come when we're through in here."

Denise must have been used to a lot of verbal abuse. She just smiled, nodded her head, and shut the door.

"When did Lionel get the combination?"

"When I was in Europe. I called him. Gave him instructions. I wanted certain packages sent to me."

"You gave him the combination on the phone?"

He snorted through his nose. "I'm not stupid, Polo. I used this." He patted the facsimile machine on his desk. "I sent Lionel a fax message. While the message was being sent, I was speaking to him on the phone. To make sure he received it, and that he was alone when he did so. There was no way anyone could have intercepted the fax message. Lionel burned it right away, while he was on the phone with me. I went so far as to have a prearranged code, so that the numbers in the message were not the actual combination numbers. I stayed on the phone and made sure he was able to open the vault."

"Had Lionel ever been in the vault before?" I said.

"Certainly. But only with me present. He'd never been in there alone before. Never."

"So who knew he had the combination?"

Martel chewed at his lip and explored my face with his eyes. "Ah, that is the question, isn't it? Lionel claims that he told no one, swears it on his life. But someone had to know, didn't they?"

"It's possible that they didn't. Just knew that the vault was there, and that there had to be something valuable in it, that Lionel knew the combination and the homeless benefit was a perfect cover to get in here and pull a burglary."

"Possible, but not probable. I think the thieves knew exactly what they were after," he said.

"The paintings."

"Exactly. The paintings."

"And the packages Lionel was shipping to you. They were paintings, too, weren't they?"

"None of your business, Mr. Polo."

I took a deep breath, letting the air hiss out between my lips. "Mr. Martel, during the Second World War you were attached to a special branch of the OSS. Part of your job was recovering works of art snatched by the Germans. Were the paintings taken from the vault some of those you came across during the war?"

His face was turning an unhealthy gray color. "Where did you get that information?"

"Sources, Mr. Martel. That was one of the reasons you hired me. My sources. A lot of long-lost paintings have turned up lately. You can't cover up things like that. The art world is a small one. Word gets around."

His voice got very low. "Have you spoken to the police about this?"

"No. Now level with me. The packages Lionel was shipping over to you. They were paintings, weren't they?"

"Yes. I own art galleries. It is not unusual that I would be shipping paintings."

"How were they shipped?"

"Lionel transported them to one of the cargo airlines. Flying Tigers at the airport. I instructed him to stay there, wait until they were loaded, and the plane took off."

"Then someone could have followed him?"

"Certainly," he agreed. "But they would have to know what he was shipping."

"What about the people who were buying the paintings in Europe. Could they be involved?"

"Impossible."

"Your wife? Was she with you in Europe?"

"Yes, the entire time."

"Then she could have known about your calls to Lionel."

"That's doubtful," he said. "I only saw her in the evenings. Her days were spent shopping and seeing the sights. Denise has very little interest in my business. I make sure of that."

"What about your daughter, Michelle?"

"What about her?"

"Would she have known what Lionel was up to?"

"I doubt it. They have never been close. She would not have had any idea what was in the vault. She was never allowed in there."

"How about business rivals? Chuck Bodine for instance."

"Bodine. Where did you get that name?"

"He was at the homeless benefit. I played cards with him and Lionel, just before the robbery."

"Bodine has no reason to be involved in something like this. None at all. And he'd never harm Lionel. He's like an uncle to the boy. My wife, my daughter, my son. None of them would have anything to gain by this stupid robbery. They all know I'd kick them out of the house and disown them. They would never take such a risk, believe me." He stood up. "And all of this speculation doesn't solve the problem. The paintings. I want them back. That is the only thing that matters. I'm willing to pay whoever took them. After we get them back, then I will get my revenge. These are ruthless men. Professional thieves. They will pay for what they did to my paintings, and for what they did to my son, but for now, the only thing that matters is getting those paintings back."

"I want to know more about those missing paintings."

"You know as much as you need to know, Mr. Polo."

"No, I don't. I don't know how many paintings were taken. I don't know their size. I don't know how they got the paintings out of here. I don't know—"

"All right, all right, I'll show you," he said harshly, getting to his feet and going over to the vault. He fiddled with the dials, then with an effort, pushed the steel door open.

The vault was really a very large room. One wall was covered with metal drawers, very much like the safety deposit room in a bank. The drawers went from ceiling to floor, small drawers on the top, graduating in size until they were three feet high on the bottom. A long oak table stood against the far wall. There were two Apple computers, a printer, two phones, and another fax machine on the table. Another table held a large adding machine. Next to the table were four metal filing cabinets.

"I conduct most of my business in here," Claude Martel said, closing the vault door behind us. He must have seen my eyes starting to pop.

"Don't worry. We're not locked in. I simply use the combination again, and the vault door unlocks. The paintings were right there," he said, pointing to the desk with the adding machine. "All wrapped and numbered. Ready to be sent to me when I notified Lionel." He held out his arms past his shoulders. "One was approximately this wide, about the same height. You saw the size of the one you got at the pier. The other was about that same size."

"All in their frames?"

"Yes, indeed. The frames are worth real money. They were made by real craftsmen in the old days. Sometimes by the artists themselves."

"How many paintings were taken the night of the robbery?"

"Three," he said, letting the word out slowly, as if each letter were costing him money.

"So that leaves two still out there. The artists?"

He shook his head. "You have no need to know."

I looked around the room slowly, learning nothing, other than that Claude Martel was a very cautious man. I walked over to the wall of metal boxes. Each had its own lock.

"Come," Martel said, "it's time for dinner."

19

Dinner was a rather somber affair, which was too bad, because the food was wonderful. The dining room table could have held thirty or more people, all with plenty of elbow and knee room. It was set in linen, with Baccarat crystal, and heavy silver cutlery.

Claude Martel sat at the head of the table, with Denise on his left, and Lionel on his right. Roy Whitman sat next to Lionel, while I was between Denise and Michelle Martel, a forewarning of things to come.

First an appetizer of chicken liver pâté, and thin slices of still-warm French bread and *cornichons*, the little green pickles that are packed in vinegar and tarragon. Then an all-white soup that had me guessing until the first sip. Cauliflower, enriched with lots of whipping cream.

The butler was doing yeoman duty in bringing out the dishes, and bottles of wine with each course, always allowing Claude Martel the first sip of wine, and waiting patiently until Martel nodded his head gravely that it was fit to drink. With the fish dish, trout with almonds, he poured a chardonnay. With the main course, lamb shoulder stuffed with ground pork, pimentos, and olives, he was pouring a red wine that was so good I kept each sip in my mouth as long as possible before swallowing.

The dinner conversation was low keyed. Lionel was having trouble eating with just one hand, even though someone in the kitchen had carefully cut up all of his food before serving it.

Claude Martel remained silent, answering the few questions spoken in his direction with grunts. Whitman sat and ate, watching the others' movements so he didn't pick up the wrong fork or spoon. With that kind of food, there is no wrong fork or spoon.

Denise and Michelle leaned across me to carry on a conversation about the latest fashions. They also kept their feet and knees busy bumping into mine. They acted like the best of friends, hardly the portrait Michelle had painted at my place earlier in the afternoon.

Claude Martel excused himself after the lamb dish, and the mood lightened after he was gone from the room.

"Lionel, darling," Denise said. "That must be dreadful for you. So much trouble just eating. How ever do you shave or shower?"

Lionel blushed lightly, and before he could respond, Michelle popped in, "Or go to the bathroom." Both women found this to be hilarious and started to giggle.

Dessert was brought in, chocolate ice cream with shaved chocolate sprinkled on top.

"You have a wonderful appetite, Mr. Polo," Michelle said. "How do you stay so trim?"

I looked at Whitman and said, "I swim a lot."

Denise went into her giggling act.

Lionel stood up and said something about seeing his father.

The girls didn't touch their dessert either, and both got up, continuing their fashion conversation.

I dug into my ice cream.

"What have you been up to, Polo?" Whitman asked.

"Not much. How about you?"

He leaned back on his chair, balancing on the rear legs. "Old man Martel's got me hanging around waiting for the next call. Pain in the ass." He used a thumbnail to dig for something between his front teeth. "Can't really complain though," he said after pulling out his thumb and wiping it on the tablecloth. "The meter's running. As long as Martel is paying, what the hell."

"Thanks for the use of your jacket. I left it in Martel's office." I looked him in the eyes. "Your notepad is still in it."

"Thanks," he said, taking a final sip of coffee. "I think I'll go see what the old man is up to."

So I was alone with my ice cream, wondering about Whitman, about his having Chuck Bodine on his Rolodex, and about the favor he'd done to get in the good graces of Lionel Martel. The butler came in and started cleaning up. "Anything else, sir?" he asked with a slight chill in his voice.

"No, thank you. But my compliments to the kitchen. That was a superb meal."

That got me a slight nod, and as he was picking up the plates, a question. "Would you care for an after-dinner drink, sir?"

"I'd love another glass of that red wine."

He was back a couple of minutes later with a bottle, about three-quarters full. He poured and put the bottle down and went about his cleaning chores. I examined the label: 1970 Château Petrus, St.-Émilion. I took my time finishing my glass.

"Good, isn't it, sir?" said the butler.

"Better than anything I've tasted before, I think." I looked around. We were still alone. "Can I pour you a glass?"

"Not necessary. I'm in charge of the wine cellar, sir," he said with a slightly superior look.

I would put up with a lot of door answering and serving of food and Claude Martel's bad temper to be in charge of that cellar.

I went back to Martel's office for a while, but was getting tired of inhaling his cigar smoke. Roy Whitman was camped in a corner of the room reading a book. I couldn't make out the title.

"I think I'll turn in early," I told Martel. "You can always call me if something comes in."

He nodded and pushed a button on his desk. "Charles will show you to your room."

Within a minute my butler friend came arunning.

At least I knew his first name now. Charles took me up the staircase, past Denise Martel's room, and down a long corridor.

"I think you'll be comfortable here, sir," Charles said, opening the door for me. "If you need anything, simply push number seven on the phone."

Compared to the rest of the house, it wasn't much. Compared to what I lived in, it wasn't too shabby. The walls were beige, and I wasn't sure just what they were covered with until I felt them. Flannel. Who the hell ever thought of flannel walls? There were floor-to-ceiling oak shutters over the windows. The bed was raised on a little platform. The bedspread and pillows were dark brown, with beige striping. Directly over the bed was a painting, what else? This was an oil, with some long, skinny dogs jumping up on a wooden table where a pair of dead rabbits lay. The bedside lamps were Oriental, twisted gargoyles that looked like something out of a Steven Spielberg movie. There was a TV with a remote control across from the bed.

I flipped through channel after channel, stopping at a news special featuring Sam Donaldson. I wondered if he had inherited his toupee from Howard Cosell, or if it was an original. I dozed off during a John Wayne flick, took a quick shower, and decided to call it a night.

I was under the covers and back into the Wayne movie when there was a knock on the door, and then Denise Martel came in. She was carrying a bottle of red wine.

"I noticed you enjoyed this at dinner, Nick," she said, putting the bottle down and sliding into bed.

So much for John Wayne.

I was wakened by Denise's massaging my back. I started to turn around, but she said, "Lie there. Relax, enjoy."

I did. Her hands felt wonderful, on my back, shoulders, ankles, calves. I sat up with a jolt. That was two hands too many. When I turned over, there was Denise, and behind her was the lean, naked body of Michelle Martel. Thus began the ménage à Martel. I protested at first, I really did, but I was outnumbered, and soon the bed was filled with twisting bodies, legs, arms, and all other vital parts moving around in a topsy-turvy symphony of lecherousness.

After having, shall we say, petered out, the ladies went at it alone, and I got the distinct feeling that Michelle preferred it that way. I slipped out of bed and shuffled to the bathroom, looking at myself in the mirror and not much liking what I saw. What the hell could you do? I asked myself rationally. Leave? Kick them out of their own house? Tell them that the sainted nuns of St. Peter and Paul's, while never going into specifics, definitely hinted that what we had done was really a no-no? Stomped out of the room naked and protested to Claude Martel—"Claude, your wife and daughter are jumping my bones, and I'm getting sick and tired of it?" My eyes met my eyes in the mirror again. And tell the truth, Polo, you enjoyed it, didn't you? I switched off the light before the mirror could answer me.

I opened the door and trod softly into the room, looking for the chair with my clothes. Sunlight was starting to stream through the shutters. One of the girls got up from the bed. It was Michelle. She stooped down to pick up a nightgown, slipped it on, walked over to me, and slapped my face.

"Prick," she said loudly, then strode out the door.

I sat down on the edge of the bed, rubbing my cheek where she'd slapped me.

Denise Martel's hand joined mine.

"Did I hear someone say 'prick'?" she said.

20

Another shower, this one blessedly alone. Then I dressed quickly while Denise was dreaming away the morning. I made sure I was completely dressed before nudging her awake.

"Shouldn't you leave before the maid gets here?" I said.

She smiled and reached out to me.

I backpedaled. "I've got to see a man. Claude Martel. You know him, I think."

She stuck a long, pink tongue out at me, then pulled the pillow over her head.

Charles the butler was in the dining room, presiding over the table, which was covered with a half dozen heavy silver warming trays.

"Breakfast, sir. There's ham, sausage, bacon, scrambled eggs, and cottage potatoes. If you prefer something else, I'll talk to the cook."

"No, Charles. That will be fine. I'll help myself. Do you know where Mr. Martel is?"

"In his office, sir."

I filled a plate with ham and eggs. A linen-covered basket held a mixture of rolls and buttered cinnamon toast. The coffee was a deep, rich French roast. I was the only customer. I wondered what they did with their leftovers.

After scraping the plate, I carried a cup of coffee into Martel's office. He was smoking again, and the ashtray in front of him held the short stubs of two cigars. He needed a shave and was wearing the same jacket and shirt he'd had on last night.

"No one called," he protested.

"Where's Whitman?" I asked.

Martel upturned a palm. "In his room, I would imagine. He didn't leave the house last night, I can assure you of that."

Which meant Martel had Whitman's room watched. I wondered how close Whitman's room was to mine, and what the watcher thought of the traffic in and out of my door.

"I've got a few leads to check out on that waiter."

"Yes, I suggest—"

We were interrupted by a knock on the door.

Whitman came barging in.

"Mr. Martel," he said, "I just checked with my answering machine. Nothing regarding the paintings, but I've got to get back to my office." He settled into a leather chair. "Besides, it's possible that whoever took the paintings is afraid to call here. Afraid of a phone tap."

Martel took his eyes off Whitman and raised a questioning eyebrow in my direction.

"Could be," I said. "But what if they do call here, and you're away?" I asked Whitman.

"No problem." He patted his waist. "I've got a pager. All Mr. Martel has to do is call my page number and I'll get right back to him."

Martel pinched his nose between his thumb and forefinger. He didn't look convinced. Finally he said, "Mr. Polo, do you have a pager?"

"No."

He went back to the nose pinching.

Whitman was fiddling on the edge of his chair. "I've got another pager at my office." He unhooked the cigarette-package-sized plastic pager from his belt. "He can use mine."

Whitman went over the pager's directions with Claude Martel. "All you have to do is call the number shown on the pager. If it's an urgent message, after you hear a tone, just tap in six six six, that's the emergency code I use. If it's not real urgent, use three three three. Simple. I'll pick my other pager up at the office and call you with its number. Every pager has a separate number, so, if you want to get hold of just one of us, it's no problem."

Whitman handed me the pager. I hated them. Electronic puppet strings. I'd vowed never to be stuck with one of them, but under the circumstances, I didn't really have much choice.

"All right," Martel said reluctantly. The rest of his current cigar joined the stubs in the ashtray. "But I want you both to stay close enough so that you can get back here right away when a call comes in."

Whitman shook Martel's hand, reminded me to be careful with the pager, then took off.

"What do you think?" Martel asked when the door closed behind Whitman. "Is it worth following him?"

"No. He'll be on the lookout for a tail. And he'll use a pay phone to call his contact. My bet is you'll be hearing something on the paintings in a few hours."

If he didn't, then something was wrong. Either Whitman somehow wasn't involved, which I found hard to believe, or he was being squeezed out by whoever did have the paintings.

I made a quick stop at my flat for a change of clothes. There were no messages. I called my money expert in Southern California.

"I was about to call you, Polo," he said when I connected with him.

"I wanted to save you the toll charge. Anything turn up?"

"Quite a bit. Got a pencil."

"Yes." Usually I tape-record a call such as this, but this chap has an electronic device that can detect a recorder. As soon as he knows you're recording him, he'll hang up, and you'll never get into his Pandora's box again.

"Claude Martel," he said, "is having more than a spot of trouble. He overextended himself on the Pacific Rim. Hong Kong, Singapore, and Manila. What looked like good deals at the time have definitely turned sour. He was tight with both Marcos and Aquino, but as you know, things have changed over there. The sugar business is in trouble, so is the real estate market in Hong Kong. Martel got in too late. He's lost a lot of money on the Tokyo exchange. He's had to refinance a lot of his stateside properties to cover his problems." I could hear the sound of shuffling paper. "Martel, Inc. went public twelve years ago. Its high this year was fourteen and an eighth. It's down three points, and I don't think it would be a bad move to short the stock now. A lot of problems ahead. This I can't confirm, but the rumor is that there is going to be a takeover bid, after the stock drops a few more points."

"Any idea who is planning the takeover?" I asked.

"Rumors again, Polo. I have nothing but rumors."

"I'll take them."

"A man named Charles Bodine, a Texas banker. He's a minor stockholder now, but he's bought a lot of shares in his name, and the word is that some dummy corporations are buying up a lot more."

"Just how big is this Bodine?"

"You didn't ask me to check on him."

"But I'll bet you did," I said.

"You won't find out, unless you up the ante."

I sighed into the phone. "Is money all you ever think about?"

"It's why you call me."

"Okay. I'll pay. Tell me about Bodine."

"One tough cookie. A real old-fashioned Texan. Got his start in the oil business, worked the fields, married into money, when oil was king. Hedged his bets, so he didn't lose everything like a lot of oil people. He got in early on those Texas savings and loans that Uncle Sam has had to bail out. He's handled a lot of Martel's financing, both in the States and on the Pacific Rim."

"Who is the majority shareholder in Martel, Inc.?"

More shuffling of paper. "A Lionel Martel is listed as a vice president. Let's see, he's a minor player, less than five percent of the stock. Claude holds the majority, just over fifty percent."

"And Bodine?"

"He's listed as the treasurer. Ten percent. Of course this doesn't count what he's been snapping up on the market."

"What about Denise or Michelle Martel?"

"No mention of them in corporate or company banking records. Here's something that might be of interest to you, Polo. Claude Martel did some fancy refinancing of some San Francisco property recently. Seems he's in need of cash. And I mean real cash, the green kind you carry in your wallet. Except you'd need a real big wallet for this amount of government issue. We're talking millions. And speaking of money, pal, drop the check in the mail today."

Cash. So Claude Martel was getting ready to pay for his paintings. I was glad to see that even a man of his wealth was having trouble digging it up. You just didn't walk into your friendly neighborhood bank and ask for a few million in cash. Even if you had that much in your account, the bank would have to make arrangements with the Federal Reserve Bank to have that much ready green available.

I called Inspector Paul Paulsen and begged another favor. "Paul, if you're by your computer, run a local criminal check on Roy Whitman for me."

"Whitman?" Paulsen asked in a suspicious voice. "Old

hand-in-your-pocket Whitman? What's he been up to lately?"

"That's what I'm trying to find out."

"Hold on," Paulsen said.

Which I did, using the time to write out a check for the information on Martel and Bodine.

"He's been a good boy," Paulsen said when he came back on the line. "At least he hasn't got caught at anything in the last nine years. Just that one arrest, no conviction on those burglary charges."

"What's the criminal action number on that case."

Paulsen read me the number. "You know," Paulsen said, "I saw Whitman down here about a year or so ago. He was with Marty Bastiani. They didn't seem to be getting along very well."

"Bastiani still a lieutenant in Vice?"

"Yeah, he's still there."

I thanked him and scheduled a lunch for next week.

"Give me a day's warning," he said. "I want to make sure I come real hungry."

My police inspector badge came in handy again at the doors of the Hall of Justice. There was a line of characters, everything from pin-striped attorneys with Gucci briefcases to people three days in need of a shave and four of a bath, waiting to get through the metal detector. A bored uniformed cop checked their baggage and repeated his chorus of, "All metal objects and cigarettes on the table before going through the machine, please," as each new visitor approached the electronic archway. I flashed my badge and walked around the crowd and into the lobby. There was the usual morning rush of people hurrying to see their probation officer, their public defender, and eventually, their judge and jury.

The first thing you have to learn about any Hall of Justice is not to use the elevators. You can go into one of those smelling of clean soap and shampoo, of expensive perfume or after-shave, and get out one floor later smelling like something the garbage man tells you to wrap in a separate container next time or he won't pick up at your place anymore.

I trudged up four flights of stairs and went to the Vice Detail. The secretary at the outer office didn't know me from Adam, so I had to give her my name and ask to speak to Lieutenant Bastiani.

Bastiani came out to greet me a few minutes later. He's a big, burly guy with black hair so thick he has to struggle to get a comb through it. We had worked together in the Fraud Detail some years back and had had some good times together, mostly at North Beach restaurants. For such a big man, he had soft, delicate hands, and he could butter a piece of French bread, or spear the last ravioli from a platter, with all the grace and delicacy of a brain surgeon.

He escorted me to his office, and we shared a few white lies about how neither had aged a day since our last meeting.

"What's up, Nick?" Bastiani asked once we were in his office behind a closed door.

"Roy Whitman, Marty. I'm working on something for a client, and I think Whitman is putting the screws into him."

His face lost its friendly look. "Whitman? That bastard. How are you connected to him?"

"My client is a man named Claude Martel. Whitman supposedly did some kind of a job for his son, Lionel."

Bastiani hitched his pants up and said, "Oh, he did a job for him all right. Remember the lollypop whorehouse bust?"

I did indeed. Some lowlifes were running a house of prostitution in the Mission District. The girls' ages ranged between twelve and sixteen. Some heavyweights had been busted, including a prominent politician. One of the girls identified him after seeing his face on TV. The newspapers had a field day with the story. There were lots of juicy rumors about certain well-known regular customers who hadn't been arrested.

I said, "You mean that Whitman got Lionel Martel off the hook on that one?"

"Whitman was representing a couple of guys," Bastiani said. "We had enough evidence to prosecute, but the girls suddenly developed amnesia about them. Whitman got to them, bought them off, I'd bet my badge on it."

"You say Whitman represented a couple of guys. Let me make a guess. Was the other one named Bodine?"

"That's the name, Nick. If you get a chance to stick a knife into Whitman's back, give it a little twist for me."

I told Bastiani I'd do all I could to accommodate him, then walked down one flight of stairs to the Superior Court Criminal Clerk's Office. There were four clerks behind the counter, none of whom I knew. I asked for the file number Paulsen had given me and was told that it was in storage.

"Fill out a form," a bored gentleman in his fifties told me, pointing to a open-topped cardboard box, "and it will be available in about four days."

Out came the old badge. "Sorry to trouble you, but we need it today."

He gave me a tired smile. "I'll be right back, Inspector."

Right back turned out to be about a half hour later. The manila file was thick, the yellowing paper covered with scribbled notes. I leaned on the counter and thumbed through the file, which contained the booking sheet, the district attorney's report, the probation report, and the various court filing documents, ending with one showing that the suspect, Roy Whitman, was found not guilty. All of which I knew. What I didn't know were the names of the guys who had been arrested with Whitman. The DA report not only showed their names, but their San Francisco criminal ID number.

I copied down the names: Kenneth Robsen and Patrick Lanagan, and the ID numbers. I paged through the large indexed criminal volumes from 1984 to the present and checked both names. By the way, if you're concerned about the gentleman with the pierced nose, blue hair, and customized van with a waterbed who's been calling on your daughter, or the neighbor who always seems to have his telescope zeroed in on your bedroom window, by all means go down to your local courthouse and check him out through the criminal indexes. They are public records, even if the clerks sometimes act as if they're handing you the plans to the Stealth bomber.

Lanagan had several arrests, the last three years ago on a burglary charge.

Robsen had been busted less than a year ago, for armed robbery.

I had the clerk pull both files. Robsen had been convicted and given a fifteen-year sentence. Even with extreme good behavior, he should still be a guest at a state-run crossbar hotel.

Lanagan had been convicted on the burglary charge and given five years.

I used the pay phone near the elevators to call Inspector Paul Paulsen again. He was "out on a case," which meant he could be gone for the rest of the day. Cops are "out on a case" like lawyers are "in a meeting."

That meant back up one flight of stairs up to the fourth floor again and the Criminal Records Division.

Another line of people, looking almost identical to the ones waiting in front of the metal detector, were now queued up to get accident reports, ID cards, or copies of their own criminal records.

I bypassed the line and went to an open window with the sign POLICE OFFICERS ONLY painted in black on the grimy glass partition.

Again there was no one that looked familiar. I filled out the necessary form, signing my name "Inspector A. Goodman." "Archie" may have been pushing it. A clerk, a pretty brunette no more than twenty-one, in a tight red sweater and designer jeans, eventually wandered over. "Yeah, whatcha need?" she asked in a voice distorted by the gum she was chewing.

I shoved the slip through the small slit in the glass. "Mug shots, darling. On both of them."

Nobody ever looks like Paul Newman in a mug shot, not even Newman if he were unfortunate enough to be booked for selling spaghetti sauce under false pretenses (stick to the acting Paul), and Kenneth Robsen was no exception. A long thin face, with a hooking nose and receding curly blond hair.

But Robsen looked like Robert Redford compared to Patrick Lanagan. Old dirty-nails himself. The waiter who had led Lionel Martel away from the poker game.

21

Back to the stairs, but only as far as the third floor, and the Adult Probation Department. Joel Loomis was in my recruit class when I went into the police department. He was a lean, hard-muscled guy with a crew cut then. Most of the crew had bailed out now, and the muscles had turned soft. He had lasted four years in the police department, became disenchanted, and gone into Probation. He had the look of a man waiting for the magic day when he could retire.

We exchanged pleasantries, then Loomis asked, "What can I do for you, Nick?"

I gave him the information on Lanagan. "I need an address."

"You sure he's not still in prison?"

"Positive. I saw him a couple of days ago."

"Okay, let's see what we've got on him."

He swiveled around so he could get at his desktop computer and punched in commands slowly with the index fingers of both hands. Green letters began flashing across the screen. He punched some more commands, grunted, then stood up.

"Nick, this is privileged information. I can't let you see it. I can tell you that he is in the area, and that if you want, I can write to him and advise him that you want to see him."

He walked over to me, leaned over my shoulder, and whispered in my ear, "I wouldn't bet that the fuckers don't have the whole building bugged."

I said, "Thank you for your cooperation, Mr. Loomis," shook his hand, then bent over the desk and looked at the computer. Lanagan's listed address was a hotel on Eddy Street. Employment was shown as the Salvation Army.

I called the Salvation Army, telling them I was Lanagan's probation officer. They hadn't seen or heard from him in weeks.

The Richman Hotel hadn't had a rich man as a guest in a long time, unless you assumed that Pat Lanagan had Martel's paintings stashed under his bed. It catered to old retired seamen and recent ex-cons. It, like almost all the old residence hotels in the Tenderloin District, was run by Indians, not the cowboys-and kind, but the Calcutta, Bombay kind.

The manager greeted me politely. I asked for Lanagan. He checked his record book.

"Mr. Lanagan moved out two weeks ago, sir. He did not leave a forwarding address."

I took out my badge, which I was flashing more now than I did when I was in the department. "Did he have any particular friends in the building."

"No, sir. Not that I know of, he was a very quiet man. I hardly saw him."

"Which room was his?" I asked.

"Room five twenty-five."

I used the elevator, until the smell made me stop at the third floor. Bad move. The stairways reeked of urine and spoiled food. I made it up to the fifth floor and began knocking on doors.

No flashing the badge here. I just held up Lanagan's mug shot and said I was looking for him. Most of the tenants were old-timers who politely listened to my spiel, but had no news. Several were hard-faced younger men who started shaking their heads no before I opened my mouth.

I was down to the second floor and in need of a shot of pure oxygen to clear my lungs. The man who answered the knock to room 208 looked like a department-store Santa Claus. He had long white hair and a long white beard, yellowing around his nose and mouth. What was visible of his face were lined and sunken cheeks and a nose with pockmarks the size of BBs. He had watery blue eyes, which he blinked a lot. He was wearing baggy old Big Ben pants, held up by thick suspenders, and a thermal undershirt.

"What can I do for you, young fellow?" he asked cheerfully.

I showed him Lanagan's picture. "I'm trying to find Pat."

The eyes started blinking even faster. "What for, may I ask?"

"I just want to ask him some questions."

"Lanagan was never a man who liked answering questions."

"Then you know him, Mr.—"

"Oh, yeah. I know him. Well as anyone around here, I guess. Come on in."

There was just one room; a bed, a battered chair with the stuffing hanging out, a TV with twisted rabbit ears, and a two-burner hot plate. Something was cooking in a grimy metal pot. It smelled awful. There was an opened can of Alpo dog food next to the pot.

"When's the last time you saw Lanagan?"

His hand ruffled his beard. "Oh, a week or so ago. On his boat."

"Lanagan's got a boat?"

"Sort of."

I took out my wallet. "How do I know you're telling me the truth?"

"Well, when you get to the boat and see Lanagan, you'll know, won't you, young fella?"

I pulled out a fifty-dollar bill and dropped it on his bed. "Where's the boat?"

He picked up the bill and rubbed it between his hands, as if he wanted to warm it up. "It's more of a houseboat really. Down on Islais Creek. You can't miss it—big, square thing, painted black and yellow. Has a little outboard, white one, tied up alongside it."

"And you were there about a week ago?"

"Yeah, about that. I don't keep too close a track on time anymore. I helped Lanagan move. He's got an old beat-up VW van. Was white once, I guess. Side door is all smashed in. Helped him with that little pisser of an outboard. He don't know much about the water, Patrick, he sure don't."

"But you do?"

"Damn right, I do. I did a lot of sailin' in my day, fella. A lot."

"Just what did you show Lanagan?"

"Showed him how to run that little pisser of a boat. Mostly I told him what not to do. People use a boat like that, think they can go cruising around the Bay, like a car on a freeway. It's not like that, I can tell you. The Bay can be as rough as water a couple of hundred miles out the Gate. Treat water with respect, I told him. Any water."

"Do you think Lanagan's still at this houseboat?"

He scratched his stomach. "Don't know. Don't care really."

"Have you got a dog?" I asked him.

"No, can't keep dogs in the hotel."

I dropped another fifty on the bed. "Why don't you eat out tonight?"

22

Islais Creek actually used to be a creek and if I remembered my high school history classes, supplied the city with some of its much-needed water around the middle of the last century. It's a dirty channel of water now that runs for a length of about three blocks, out to China Basin in the San Francisco Bay.

It's bordered by a freeway on one side, and warehouses on the other, and has two small drawbridges spanning it, one on Fourth Street, the other, the Lefty O'Doul Bridge, on Third Street, named after the great San Francisco baseball legend.

On a busy day the bridges get raised two or three times, and then only after the boatman gives the bridgemaster an hour's warning. If the tides are right, a small boat can scoot right under the bridges, with little more than headroom for clearance.

There's a restaurant, Carmen's, next to the Fourth Street Bridge, and a block or so away, a drive-in hamburger stand whose claim to fame is that Clint Eastwood filmed one of his Dirty Harry pictures there. The one where Harry mutters his famous line: "Go ahead, make my day!"

Islais Creek is not the greatest location in town, but it is only a five-minute walk, or ten-minute boat ride, to the Mission Rock Resort.

I parked in a gravel-topped lot abutting the water, alongside a battered VW van, with the passenger-side door crumpled in, just like the old-timer had described it. A pack of six or seven cats was picnicking in a garbage Dumpster near the small wooden bridge that connected to the steps leading down to the boat dock. There were some thirty or so boats and houseboats tied up along the dock. Most looked like permanent fixtures; living quarters that just happened to be on the water, rather than on land. One houseboat was simply a trailer, tied down to a barge. Another was painted black, with yellow trim, and had a small, white outboard tied up next to it. Score another one for my Santa Claus friend.

I took the .32 revolver out of its holster, crossed the small wooden bridge, and goose-stepped over some good-sized dog droppings. The wood planking was worn and cracked. The piling posts were covered with thick green slime, and the dark water had an oily sheen on it. Some of the boats seemed to be in pretty good repair, but none of them had to worry about a visit from Robin Leach's television crew.

There was no visible number or mailbox on the black houseboat. The windows were covered from inside with bamboo shades. The front door had a small glass peephole at eye level. I stood there for a minute, listening for any movement from inside, then knocked on the door and edged a few feet away, keeping my eye on the bamboo shades. I knocked again, with my left hand, since my right was cradling the revolver. Nothing. No one seemed to be paying attention to me, but it was too light to try anything fancy. I did give the doorknob a little turn, but in real life, they're always locked. This one was no exception.

I retreated to my car and considered the options. If the old man at the hotel hadn't been giving me a line, the houseboat was Lanagan's new address. And there was even a possibility that Martel's paintings were inside. Breaking into the place in broad daylight was going to be a problem. It is a fact that daytime burglaries far outnumber nighttime burglaries. It is a lesser-known fact that there are more daytime burglars in jail than nighttime burglars. Besides, my friend with the taste for dog food might just be giving me the runaround, and the houseboat really belonged to one of his cronies and not to Lanagan.

I backed my car down the street and used the pay phone in Carmen's restaurant to call Martel.

"Whitman's our man," I told him. "No doubt about it. The waiter, the one that led Lionel away from the card game, is a longtime con. He just got out of jail. A few years back he was arrested with Whitman on a burglary charge. Whitman got off, he didn't."

"The man's name?" Martel asked.

"Lanagan. Patrick Lanagan."

"And you're sure Whitman knows him?"

"Positive. They were partners. Lanagan went to jail, Whitman didn't. There's no way Lanagan could have been at the party without Whitman's seeing him."

"Let me think," Martel said. I could hear the click of his lighter and almost expected cigar smoke to come through my phone.

"Where are you calling from?" he finally asked.

"At a restaurant on Islais Creek. I'm pretty sure it's where Lanagan is living now, on a houseboat, but no one's home, or at least no one's answering the door."

"Then the paintings may be there now!"

"It's a possibility."

"Can't you find out?" Martel said in a demanding tone.

"I can't break in there without being spotted, and I'm not absolutely positive that this is where Lanagan's living. If I were sure the paintings were in there, it'd be worth the risk."

"You're afraid of this scum?" Martel said sarcastically.

"Lanagan's no patsy. I may want to take piano lessons one of these days. Remember what he did to Lionel."

"What do you suggest, then?"

"Wait for them to make their move. You keep telling me your prime concern is the paintings. Get them safely back, now that we know for sure who's involved."

Martel agreed. I made a quick pit stop at the restaurant men's room, then ordered a San Miguel beer and a bowl of *abado,* the great Filipino stew they make by boiling the pork in vinegar and water and then giving it a quick sauté.

The dock in back of Carmen's restaurant stretched out a good fifty yards and was covered with tables, benches, and an odd assortment of potted cactus and succulent plants. The black houseboat was easily visible. If you had to pull a surveillance job, this is the way to do it.

I was on my second San Miguel when the beeper on my hip started its annoying noise. The pager's readout was showing the numbers 666. Martel's panic signal.

A big, heavy-set man in work pants and a gimme hat with the name CATERPILLAR TRACTOR on it was using the restaurant's pay phone. He didn't look to be in a hurry.

I waved a twenty-dollar bill under his nose. "I really need the phone," I told him.

He smiled broadly. "I guess you do, pal." He handed me the receiver.

I dialed Claude Martel's number.

"Whitman called," Martel said. He sounded winded, as if he'd been jogging with Michelle. "He says he's been contacted. That the pickup will be this afternoon. He's coming now for the money. They want three million dollars. It's less than I thought. You follow him and—"

"He won't allow a tail, believe me."

"Damn it!" Martel said hotly. "All right. You come here. Now. I want you here when I give him the money."

I headed straight for Martel's house. He was in his usual place, behind his desk, and behind a cloud of cigar smoke.

128

Two good-sized brown leather satchels, the kind that doctors used to carry in the days they made house calls, sat on the corner of the desk.

"The money?" I asked.

He nodded his head solemnly. "Three million dollars."

I sat there drooling. Whitman came in a few minutes later. He pulled up short when he saw me. "They said that Polo was definitely not to be involved, Mr. Martel."

"He won't be. He's here to witness the fact that I'm giving you the money." Martel stood up and snapped open the top of one of the satchels. "Both of you take a look."

It looked wonderful. I'd never seen that much cash.

Whitman said, "If you don't mind, sir, I'd like to open both bags. Make sure there are no transmitters. It's my ass that's on the line out there."

Martel gave him an icy smile. "Be my guest."

Whitman spilled the money on the desk. I had to give him full credit for chutzpah. He checked out the first bag thoroughly, then riffed through the stacks of money one by one as he dropped them into the satchel.

The bills were all hundreds, neatly banded together in groups of ten thousand dollars.

I did a little mental arithmetic. Each bill weighs about 1 gram. There are roughly 30 grams in an ounce, making it 480 grams a pound; 480 hundred-dollar bills would be $48,000. Wishing that I had spent more time in school studying math tables rather than Molly Fisher's budding figure, I tried to figure out just how much a million dollars would weigh. Ten pounds should come out to $480,000. Twice that, or twenty pounds' worth, made it a little under a million. So, for a round figure, and what a nice round figure it was, each million bucks weighed in somewhere close to twenty pounds.

Poor baby Whitman was risking a hernia lugging the sixty pounds of cash out the door.

Claude Martel's eyes were shooting daggers into Whitman the whole time he went through the money and the satchels.

"It looks fine," Whitman said after the last greenback was back in its satchel.

"Where is the transfer to take place?" Martel asked.

Whitman hefted one of the satchels in his hand. "I really don't know. They told me to drive around town. They'd call on my car phone and give me directions."

Martel walked over to Whitman, stretched up to his full height, and said, "If I do not get those paintings back, you are a dead man. I will have you killed, sir. Make no mistake about it. Understand?"

Whitman had probably been threatened by a hundred people during his checkered career. But never anyone with as much money as Martel. And that's one rule that never changes. Money means power.

Whitman's Adam's apple bobbed a couple of times. "I understand, Mr. Martel. You'll get your paintings."

23

As soon as Whitman was out the door, Martel came over to me. He was taking deep breaths, trying to compose himself. Finally he said, "Polo, I want the money back. Once I get the paintings, I want the money back from that no-good bastard." He made a fist of his right hand and pounded it against his thigh. "Get me the money, and a hundred thousand of it is yours. No questions asked. Understand?"

There he went with the "understand" again. Couldn't he say "savvy" or "comprehend" or "get the picture" once in a while? Whatever, I had no trouble in grasping his intention.

"A hundred thousand dollars," I mumbled, something I could certainly understand.

By the time I got outside, Whitman's car was nowhere in sight. I did my best to check for a tail and got back to Islais Creek as soon as possible. There was no sign of Whitman's Lincoln. The old beat-up VW was parked in the same spot.

I backed my car in between two empty, sixteen-wheel trailers in front of a drayage company's loading dock. My good camera with the telephoto lens was back at the flat, but my spare, a miniature Rollei, was in the car's trunk. It was great for using in places where cameras weren't supposed to be allowed, but didn't have a lens that was really suitable for long-distance, outdoor work. I loaded it with film, noticing that the expiration date on the film package was stamped six months ago. I said a silent prayer to St. Kodak, set the camera's depth-of-field scale on infinity, and found a spot that gave me a good view of the black-and-yellow houseboat. And waited.

And waited. Either the batteries in my Timex were running down, or time was moving as slowly as a Woody Allen dramatic movie.

I divided the time between fiddling with the camera's light-aperture setting, and dancing from one foot to the other, wondering if I had time to run to the restaurant's men's room.

Finally Whitman's black Lincoln pulled into the parking area. Whitman got out, slammed the door behind him, and walked rapidly to the little bridge leading to the pier. He wasn't carrying a satchel, or anything else.

I started clicking away with the Rollei as he crossed the bridge and sprinted toward the houseboat. He was barely visible through the little camera's viewing lens when he got to the door. I pulled my eye away from the camera. Whitman knocked several times on the door, then dug into his pocket and came out with a key. I went back to taking pictures as he stuck the key into the lock. The metallic clicking sound of the camera was suddenly drowned out by a deafening explosion. I dropped the camera to the ground and covered my ears with my hands, just in time, as another detonation went off.

The houseboat was covered by smoke. Pieces of wood were hurled up in the air, falling back down like huge pieces of confetti. People in the nearby houseboats were cautiously poking their heads out of windows. I ran over the bridge. A large German shepherd, his eyes wide with fear, was tugging hysterically at the rope that had him bound to one of the boats.

There was almost nothing left of the side of the houseboat where the door had been. The roof had dropped down to the ground floor in spots. The small white motorboat was still tied up to the dock, bobbing up and down in the rolling water. The mangled remains of the bottom half of a human torso lay in the bottom of the boat, the legs spread and contorted like a rag doll thrown on the floor. I put a handkerchief over my nose and mouth and entered what was left of the houseboat. Parts of the flooring were gone. I skirted a hole the size of a pool table. Something that looked like an arm and a hand was imbedded in a still-standing wall. Small fires were scattered throughout the rubble.

Someone was yelling at me, "Get out of there, mister, it's going to sink!"

The smoke had my eyes tearing. I could hear lumber groaning and looked at what was left of the roof. It was tottering slowly. I made my way out, tripping over a pile of rubble. My hand touched something slick on the floor and unconsciously jerked back. I took a closer look. There was a pile of jagged pieces of canvas, resembling a discarded jigsaw puzzle, one side untouched, the other covered with bits of color. I picked up a handful and dropped them in my pocket.

The good samaritan who'd been yelling at me grabbed me by the shoulder. "You crazy, man, going in there? The sucker's going to sink."

He was a big man, well over six feet tall, with a potbelly protruding out of a red-checkered flannel shirt.

When we were a safe distance from the burning houseboat, I asked him, "Did you know the guy who lived there, Pat Lanagan?"

"Saw him a couple of times. Redhead. Never got his name. Minded his own business. That's how most of us are down here."

A crowd was forming. I made my way back to the parking lot. Luckily, the Rollei camera was still in the gravel where I'd dropped it. The film would have the last visible evidence of the existence of Roy Whitman.

Two fire engines were already on the scene, and more were streaming into the parking lot. Firemen were strapping air tanks on their backs and carrying hoses down to the pier.

I leaned on Whitman's Lincoln and tried to get my wind back, then looked into the car. There was no sign of the satchel or any paintings.

I plodded over to one of the fire engines. Fire hose was spread on the ground like giant strands of spaghetti. A fireman was working on the side of the rig. There were enough chrome levers and black, plastic gauge handles to fill the cockpit of a Boeing 747. He went about his work with a calm efficiency.

"Police department," I told him. "Have you got a spare ax I can borrow for a minute?"

He gave me a wary look. "What you need it for?"

"Get into a car trunk."

He gave me another look, taking in my soot-covered clothes. "I got something better." He went back to his levers and dials for a minute, tapped a pressure gauge with his finger, and nodded in satisfaction. "Got to give the boys the right pressure in those lines, or the hose will whip them into the fucking water."

He reached into a compartment on the side of the engine and pulled out a strange-looking tool. "Chicago door opener," he said, handing it to me. There was an ax blade on one side, a sharp pick on the other, and a two-pronged claw on the opposite end.

"Make sure you bring it right back, huh, pal," the fireman said as I headed for Whitman's car.

I wedged the claw on the trunk's lid and pushed down and it popped right up. There was a spare tire, a tool pouch, and a canvas camera bag that contained just that: a camera, some telephoto lenses, and a half dozen rolls of film. No satchel and no paintings.

I used the fireman's tool to break into the VW wagon and found nothing but dirty clothes and empty beer cans.

I trudged back down to Carmen's and called Claude Martel with the bad news.

24

Inspector Robert Tehaney was the exact opposite of Jack Cusak: smart, tough, and dedicated. He had put in more years than he needed to collect full retirement benefits from the police department, but he stayed on the job because he was good at it, and he knew that he'd go nuts if he retired. He was pushing sixty, with thin, sandy hair, a perpetually mournful face, and a stomach that needed regular doses of Maalox.

He swallowed a couple of spoonfuls of Maalox, lighted up an unfiltered Lucky Strike, and said, "Nick, you are a real pain in the ass."

"You should be grateful to me, Tehaney. If I didn't tell you whose body was lying in that boat, you'd never have figured it out."

He let out a light belch. "Whitman's wallet and ID were still in his pants pocket."

"When will the pictures be developed?"

He looked at the watch on his freckled wrist. "Should be real soon. You could have made it a whole lot easier if you just came to us in the first place."

"I talked to Cusak. Told him to check on the waiter."

"Yeah," he said, picking a piece of tobacco off his lip and

dropping it into an ashtray. "You told Cusak, then your client tells him it was all a mistake, that there wasn't any theft."

"Would Cusak have acted on it if I told him that some paintings actually had been stolen? Hell, no. No complainant, no investigation, you know how it works."

"Listen, if you had—"

We were interrupted by the chirping of the phone on his desk. "Tehaney speaking," he said, blowing out a deep lungful of cigarette smoke.

He kept his faded blue eyes on me while he listened, nodding his head, saying "Okay" a few times, then, "Is that so? Okay, run them and see what you come up with."

He cradled the receiver slowly. "Looks like there was more than one person in there when the houseboat blew. Coroner's office found some remains inside. Got a good print from a hand. The prints didn't belong to Roy Whitman."

"I think I can save you some time, Bob. The odds are the prints will belong to a Patrick Lanagan. He's out on probation from San Quentin."

"The odds say that, huh?"

"Lanagan was involved with Whitman in those burglaries a few years back. He was dressed up as a waiter at the party at Martel's house, when the robbery went down."

Tehaney called the crime lab back and relayed the information on Lanagan. Then he reached for the Maalox bottle and said, "Let's have it from day one, Nick."

So I gave it to him, leaving out nothing of importance, unless you consider the Martel ladies' sexual escapades and burgling Whitman's office important. He interrupted just once.

"Interpol? Why the hell are they involved?"

"Gene Lembi, the Interpol agent, thinks that Claude Martel may have smuggled some valuable paintings out of Europe after World War Two."

"World War Two? Jesus Christ, how do you get involved in this shit?" He picked up the phone and called information, asking for the number for the Alcohol, Tobacco and Firearms branch of the Treasury. "I'm going to check with this guy Lembi. Take a hike for a few minutes, will you, Nick?"

I walked down to the bathroom and tried scrubbing off some of the dark stains from my hands. My sport coat was a mess and smelled like one of Tehaney's ashtrays. I used a pay phone in the hall and called Claude Martel. He hadn't been happy with my last call, from Carmen's, when I told him about the bomb, and Whitman's showing up without his paintings or money.

"Where are you?" he demanded.

"The Hall of Justice."

"Are you being held?"

"No. Just telling them what happened."

"I told you I did not want the police involved in this, damn it."

"You told me that before a couple of people were killed."

"A couple of people? You just told me about Whitman. Who else was killed?"

"The police found the remains of another body in the houseboat. The fingerprints weren't Whitman's. I'm betting they're Patrick Lanagan's."

He said something in French that I didn't understand. "You have botched this from the beginning, Polo." His voice had been reasonably calm at the start of this little conversation; it had an edge of panic in it now. "I want those paintings. And I want my money. I just have your word for it that Whitman didn't have the money and paintings with him. If Whitman didn't have them, then who does? I'll tell you who I think does. You, you bastard! You were in it with him! From the start! Bring me back those paintings, or you are dead! Understand!" The last sentences came out in a harsh shout. The sound of the phone's receiver hitting the cradle sounded like a small bomb's going off.

Tehaney was waiting for me back at his desk. He looked as if he'd just seen Notre Dame lose a football game by forty points.

"I tried getting in touch with this Lembi. Seems he just uses the Alcohol, Tobacco and Firearms office as a phone and letter drop. They haven't seen or heard from him in a couple of days. Funny thing though, they said that another San Francisco cop called for Lembi the other day: Mike Wilcox. I just called Wilcox. He said he never heard of Lembi and the only thing he knows about Interpol is what he sees in James Bond movies. So just what the hell is going on, Nick, I don't—"

Blessedly the phone interrupted us again.

"Crime lab," he said when he hung up. "They've developed your pictures. Let's go take a look."

The crime lab was on the same floor as the homicide detail, so we were there in a matter of minutes. A technician, looking like a doctor in his white smock, handed Tehaney a manila envelope.

"I blew them up as much as possible, Inspector. If there is anything you want to zero in on, just mark it with pencil and we'll see what we can do."

Tehaney opened the envelope and placed the pictures on a counter. They had come out quite well. Whitman's features were easily visible in the shots of him leaving his car and hurrying down the dock. The final one, which was taken at almost the exact same millisecond as the explosion, actually showed the flash of fire starting behind the houseboat door.

"That's Whitman all right," Tehaney said. He made a quick sign of the cross with his index finger. "Poor bastard."

"I'd like a copy of those pictures, Bob."

"Why?"

"Just to keep in my file."

He gave me a suspicious look.

"Bob, they're my pictures, I took them with my camera.

I'm happy to cooperate with the police, but I think I'm entitled to a set of the pictures."

He went into a long discourse about the rights of the police in a criminal investigation.

The technician came over while Tehaney was giving his law-and-order spiel.

"Inspector, we checked prints on the man whose name you gave us, Patrick Lanagan. It was him all right."

Tehaney grunted, looked at me, then back at the technician. "Could you make me another copy of these prints right away, please?"

I spent another half hour with Tehaney. He got a call from Donnie Hansen of the police bomb squad. Hansen was at Islais Creek and he wanted to talk to me.

There were still several fire engines in the parking lot. The fireman had done a good job; the remains of the houseboat were still on top of the water.

Hansen is a broad-shouldered guy in his forties, and the department's expert on explosive devices. He had an open wooden evidence box at his feet. I could see a shoe, what looked like pieces of a revolver, and a still-shiny stainless steel knife. The knife had a clip on the back so you could hang it on your shirt pocket. The blade was extended and looked like the retractable type that slides up into the handle when not in use. They're popular with paramedics.

Hansen saw me staring. "Amazing what kind of stuff survives an explosion, isn't it?" he said. He was wearing rubber hip boots over a grimy pair of dark coveralls. He took off his rubber gloves and shook my hand.

"I hear you were here when the bombs went off, Nick."

"Right." I handed him the set of photos that Tehaney had given me. "I was taking pictures of Whitman when it blew."

He spread the pictures across the hood of my car. He barely glanced at the ones of Whitman walking, but studied the print that showed the start of the explosion for a good two minutes.

"Did you see him put a key in the door?"

"Yes, then when he tried to open it, the place blew apart."

"The debris caused by the explosion, describe it."

"Not much to describe, Donnie, just big hunks of lumber flying through the air."

Hansen's eyebrows knitted together. "Yeah, that's all I've found, big stuff."

"Does that mean anything?"

"Ties in with everything else I've found so far." He took his eyes away from the photographs and looked at me. "What's your interest in all this, Nick? What was your action with Whitman?"

"Civil case, Donnie. Whitman was supposed to be the go-between man in recovering some items that were taken from my client's house."

Hansen made a wry face. "Sounds like Whitman." He started gathering up the photographs.

"That's my set. The crime lab has the negatives."

He handed the pictures back without comment.

"Any idea of how it went down?" I asked.

"Yeah, we're getting a pretty good picture. From the size of the debris and the explosion patterns, it looks like dynamite. You heard two explosions?"

"Right. One almost on top of the other."

"Uh-huh. Poor old Whitman unlocks the door, turns the handle. Opening the door brings together two contact points. Probably two sticks of industrial dynamite, which are about forty percent nitroglycerin. Simple setup. All that's needed is some wire, contact points, and a battery. The second blast was hooked up on a minidelay to the one at the door."

"How can you be sure it was dynamite?" I said.

"Can't be positive yet, but we'll probably find a few scraps of the stick wrappings. They never all get blown away, that's why it's a good thing the fire boys kept the barge from going under. The size of the debris points to dynamite, always bigger pieces with dynamite, it's pretty slow stuff, four hundred to eight hundred feet per second. Plastic, now that's fast, you're talking seventeen hundred to eighteen hundred feet per second with plastic, that's why it's so popular, and the debris is much smaller."

"How much expertise would the person who set this up have to have?"

"Not too much. It looks like it was a simple setup. Probably get a book on how to do it at the library."

I pointed to the old VW. "I'm pretty sure that jalopy belonged to the guy who was living in the houseboat. The black Lincoln over there was Whitman's."

Hansen slipped on his rubber gloves again. "Thanks, Nick. Time to go fishing again. Never know what you're going to find in all that shit."

25

Charles answered the door to Claude Martel's house.

"It seems you're always in need of a bath when you visit us, sir."

He didn't crack a smile at all, just kept that holier-than-thou look on his face. He opened the door wide enough for me to pass through, then said, "Mr. Martel is in his office, sir. Come with me. I'll announce you."

I liked that. Announce me. Sounded as if I were being sent in as a pinch hitter in the bottom of the ninth with the score tied.

I followed behind. He tapped sharply on the door, then opened it and said, "Mr. Polo to see you, sir."

Claude Martel was on the phone. He took one look at me, stood up, and said, "I'll call you right back," then slammed down the receiver.

"Well, what about my paintings? And my money?"

I reached into my coat pocket and took out the canvas bits I'd found on the houseboat floor and sprinkled them across his desk. "I found these after the explosion."

Martel dropped back into his chair as if his legs had been kicked out from under him. He leaned back and covered his face with his hands. "My God," he moaned, then spread his fingers and peered through them as if he were looking out from behind bars. "And the money, what about the money?"

"Whitman didn't have the money with him, I told you that. I checked his car, it wasn't there."

"Then where the hell is it, Mr. Polo?"

"I left here just a minute after Whitman did, with the money. I drove straight to Islais Creek and waited for him. I don't have a clue to where he went."

Martel leaned forward and propped his elbows on the desk. "I just have your word for that."

I handed him the envelope with the pictures.

After he had looked through them, he said, "These prove nothing. You could have met with Whitman, taken the money, and sent him along to the houseboat."

"I didn't have the time, and I don't have the knowledge, to set up two bombs, Mr. Martel. Patrick Lanagan wasn't sitting there waiting to be blown up. Whoever set up the explosives had probably killed Lanagan already."

"Yes. Whitman could have killed his partner earlier. Or you could have killed him. With or without Whitman's knowledge." He reached for the humidor and a fresh cigar. "No, you've told me nothing that makes me think you're not involved."

"If I had the money, I wouldn't be here talking to you now. And if the cops thought I had anything to do with the bombing, they'd have me in a cell."

Martel picked up one of the canvas bits, then said, "I had a call from a policeman, Inspector Tehaney. He wants to talk to me."

That would be some conversation. Between Tehaney's Lucky Strikes and Martel's cigars, they'd be lucky to see each other through the smoke.

"He's a smart cop, Mr. Martel. You won't be able to put him off, like Cusak. This is a double-homicide case. They take things like that real serious."

144

He continued to fiddle with the canvas bits, reaching into the desk drawer and bringing out a magnifying glass. He held a bit in front of the glass, examining it closely, like a butterfly whose sexual orientation he was trying to determine. He put the magnifying glass down and popped the canvas bit right into his mouth and chewed a few times, then spat the soggy mess onto the desk.

He gave me a bitter smile. "Exactly where did you find these pieces of canvas?"

"On the floor of the houseboat, right after the explosion."

"Did you pick up all of them?"

"No, they were scattered all over the place."

"Then it's quite probable that the police will find them also. If I'm any judge, the paint on that canvas is no more than a few years old. No lead. Probably acrylic. Which means that whatever paintings were blown up in that houseboat were not the ones taken from my vault."

He stood up and went over to the bar and poured two glasses of cognac, handing me one, and smiling again. "When this Inspector Tehaney interviewed you, did you tell him about the stolen paintings?"

"I didn't use the word *stolen*, I just told him that Whitman was trying to get back some missing paintings."

"Do you think he would go so far as to have his people check the paint fragments, to see their composition, how old the paint is, that kind of thing?"

"It's possible," I said.

"You didn't volunteer any information regarding just what the paintings were, did you?"

"I couldn't. You didn't tell me."

"Right." He perched on the edge of the desk and beamed down at me. "Then if he was to ask about the paintings, and I was to tell him that they were recent works, he would not be in a position to challenge me?"

"Tehaney's a bright cop, but I would think that his closest contact with painters would be with environmental abstract expressionists."

Martel looked confused.

"Housepainters."

He still looked confused.

"He wouldn't be able to challenge you," I told him. "He'll certainly check out anything you tell him with an expert, if he thinks it would be of any value in his investigation."

Martel swirled the liquor around in his glass, watching it cling to the side. I made better use of mine.

"All right, Polo," he finally said. "I'm going to give you another chance. The paintings weren't destroyed in that explosion, and obviously neither was the money. So who has them?"

"If it's not me, and it's not you, then we're down to just a couple of suspects, Chuck Bodine or Gene Lembi."

"Bodine I know. Who is this Mr. Lembi?"

"He's an agent for Interpol."

Martel raised his fanny out of the chair and leaned forward. "Interpol?"

"Yes."

"How do you know this?" Martel demanded.

"One of my sources. What about the name, Lembi? Does it mean anything to you?"

"Nothing. How old a man is he?"

"Oh, thirty-five or so. Why?"

He stared down into his drink. "I knew a man in Interpol a long time ago. So long ago I can't recall his name." His head snapped back up. "Your sources. What else do they tell you about this Lembi?"

"Not much. I know Inspector Tehaney will be talking to him."

Martel sat down and swiveled his chair so it was facing his vault. "You mentioned Charles Bodine's name." He swiveled back to face me. "Why is he a suspect?"

"Bodine was here, in your house the night of the robbery. Is it unusual for him to be in San Francisco?"

"No, not at all. He's here quite often. Keeps a condominium on Nob Hill. When he's in town, he spends a good amount of time here. We do a lot of business together."

"I know. He's holding some paper on several of your properties. Business isn't too good for you lately, is it?"

Martel's voice turned frosty enough to drop the temperature several degrees. "Why do you keep butting into my business when what I hired you to do is get back my paintings?"

"Bodine would have known you were in Europe, wouldn't he?"

"Yes. It was no secret, but I don't believe Bodine would get involved in something like this. He has been a partner, and a friend, and he's nobody's fool. He's very close to Lionel. Like an uncle. He'd never allow something like that to happen to Lionel. No, I don't see—"

We were interrupted by the phone's ringing. Martel picked it up without saying a word, listened for a few seconds, then said, "Five minutes," and hung up.

"Your policeman, Tehaney, is at the door."

"I think it's better if I leave without his seeing me, Mr. Martel. Understand?"

26

The ever-vigilant Mrs. Damonte was waiting for me when I got back to my flat. She opened her door as I started up the stairs.

"That nice man was here again," she said. "I told him you should be back later."

"'Nice man'?" I answered in my rusty Italian. "You mean Mr. Lembi?"

"Yes. He speaks beautifully," she said. Lembi better be careful. Whatever dangers he faced as an agent for Interpol would be no match for Mrs. Damonte and her ever-expanding list of nieces from Italy looking for a husband.

"When was he here?"

"During Three Stooges."

That meant between four and four-thirty when the Three Stooges were on a local TV channel. It was a sacred half hour for Mrs. D. She hated to be interrupted when Larry, Mo, and Curly were going through their antics. The Stooges, wrestling, old Mario Lanza movies, and the broadcast of the state lottery numbers were her favorites.

Her eyes wandered over my dirty clothes. "You don't look good."

I thanked her kindly and continued up the stairs to my

flat. There were three messages on the answering machine. All from Jane Tobin. All urging me to call her right away. Ah, the Polo charm again. Of course, the fact that her newspaper blood was probably on a high boil over the bomb story may have had something to do with it.

I was dialing her number when the doorbell rang. It was Jane. She was wearing white jeans, a red-and-white-striped, crew-neck T-shirt, and had a white sweater draped over her shoulders, the arms tied casually under her chin. White plastic hoop earrings, almost big enough to put your fist through, completed the outfit. She was carrying a large brown bag.

"Barbecued chicken, potato salad, and coleslaw," she said, brushing by me and heading for the kitchen.

"Store-bought salads?" I asked as she put the bag on the kitchen table.

She gave me a sidelong glance. "Of course."

Jane was a beautiful, intelligent, and talented woman; however, cooking was not one of her specialties, though she said her ex, "the bastard," had never complained about the food she served. It made me wonder about him.

She wrinkled her nose. "Why don't you shower and change your clothes, Nick? Then we can talk."

No interruptions in the shower this time, other than Jane's long arm offering a glass of wine while I was toweling off. My sport coat and slacks went in a bag for hopeful redemption at the cleaners. The suit I fell into the bay in was molding away in a similar bag. At the rate the case was going, I would be spending a good portion of my fee on wardrobe replacement. I put on a pair of old jeans and a knit shirt and carried the half-filled wineglass into the kitchen.

Jane held up her glass in a toast. "At least you look clean now." She patted the chair next to her. "Tell me what's going on, Nick. Your name has been all over the radio and TV on that bombing at Islais Creek."

I did. Sort of. Leaving out a bit, and only after we had

established the fact that all of it was off the record. Until I told her otherwise.

"So where does that leave you now?" she asked when I was finished with the story.

"With egg on my face."

Bodine seemed to be the prime suspect. Too prime?

What about Michelle Martel? Could she be a suspect? What would her connection be to Whitman? Would Michelle have heard the rumors about her father's fleeced paintings? Could he keep something like that secret from his family all those years? The gallery was a small part of Martel, Inc.'s portfolio. At least the legitimate end of it. But presumably Claude Martel's military background would be common knowledge in the family, and Michelle's elbows and knees weren't the only things sharp about her. Lembi had mentioned the paintings' being sold on the gray market. News and rumors like that spread quickly. So what if Michelle did know her father was peddling hot paintings? What would she gain by stealing them? Other than the megabucks the paintings were worth, of course. But if her father, or Claude as she preferred to call him, was in trouble and needed the money from the paintings to cover some bad business deals, would she really gain all that much if his empire collapsed? Or maybe she knew there was no hope and thought she might as well get out with the paintings at least.

Then there was Lionel. Her half brother. Would she go so far as to have his finger lopped off? She was a tough cookie, but was she that tough?

Jane waved a hand in front of my face.

"Earth to Nick," she said. "Come in Nick. You were off in another world there. What were you thinking?"

"I think you bought the skinniest chicken you could find, and salads that should have been dumped out of the delicatessen dairy case two days ago, so I'd buy you dinner."

"My, my," she said sweetly. "You really are an investigator, aren't you?"

150

We hiked down two blocks to the New Pisa, for an old-fashioned Italian dinner: minestrone soup, salad, cannelloni, chicken Toscano, and some spumone for dessert. Jane asked for a doggy bag. The waiter took the food from my plates; hers were wiped clean. We walked next door to Gino and Carlo's for a nightcap. Gino and Carlo's is a small, dark bar that serves drinks at a reasonable price and has a jukebox dominated by Sinatra. I plugged two bucks' worth of quarters in the machine, then joined Jane at the bar. She had ordered amarettos for us.

We were buzzing along nicely, getting ready to call it an evening, when someone tapped me on the shoulder. I turned to see the mystery man, Gene Lembi. He was in his gray suit and black tie outfit.

"Mrs. Damonte told me you had walked to dinner," he said. "I've been trying the restaurants up and down the street."

"Good for you," I said. "Jane Tobin, meet Gene Lembi."

Lembi gave a courteous bow and raised his eyebrows. "Jane Tobin, the reporter?"

"Columnist really. What line of work are you in, Mr. Lembi?"

I told you she was smart, didn't I? She also had a habit of switching her job title from columnist to reporter, whenever it best suited her purpose.

Lembi ignored her question, signaling to the bartender for a round of drinks. He talked about the weather until the drinks were poured, then said, "Nick, could I talk to you for just a moment?"

He walked to the end of the bar. I winked at Jane and followed him.

"You've been busy," Lembi said when we were out of Jane's hearing.

"Yes. How about you? I gave your name to Inspector

Robert Tehaney. He's handling the bombing deaths. You did hear about those, didn't you?"

"It would be impossible not to. Your name is mentioned prominently. How did Claude Martel take it?"

"Take what?"

"I've spoken to Inspector Tehaney. They've identified the two victims, Whitman and a Patrick Lanagan. He also told me there was evidence of some paintings being destroyed in the explosion." He took a quick sip of his drink. "If those were Martel's paintings, I imagine he's quite upset."

"He wasn't very happy when I spoke to him."

"Then he believes the paintings taken from him were the ones destroyed in the bombing?"

"It's a pretty good assumption," I said, looking toward the bar and seeing that a young guy in a tweed sport coat had sat down next to Jane.

Lembi's eyes followed mine. "Attractive lady. How much does she know about what's happened?"

"Hard to tell with newspaper people. I've kept her in the dark. I guess this kind of finishes off your interest in Martel."

He gave me a Cheshire cat smile. "Perhaps. I'd like to talk to you some more, Mr. Polo. Maybe we could get together tomorrow."

"Sure. I've got nothing but time now."

"I'll call you," he said, shaking my hand, then walking out of the bar.

Sure. I'll call you. Let's have lunch. Your check is in the mail. I am not a crook. All the standard clichés when you're finished with someone and want to make a hasty retreat.

The smile on the guy with the tweed jacket soured when I put my arm around Jane's shoulders and said, "Darling, don't you think it's time for us to go home and feed the twins?"

"Shame on you," Jane said when tweed coat sauntered

away. "He was such a nice young boy. What was all that secret mumbo jumbo with Mr. Lembi?"

"Just that. Mumbo jumbo. He was pumping me. That was a nice play of yours—'What line of work are you in?' Very nice indeed. Do you know anyone at the paper with connections in Paris?"

"What kind of connections?"

"The kind that could find out just how big a shot Gene Lembi is with Interpol."

"Well, I used to date Barney Ford. He's with Associated Press in Paris. I could give him a call."

"Good. Let's try it. Come on, let's go back to my place. I promised someone I'd keep you in the dark."

Sinatra was crooning "How Little We Know" as we were walking out. Very appropriate.

27

According to Jane, Paris was nine hours ahead of us, timewise, so since we got back to my flat a little after eleven, it was wake-up time in gay Paree. She ran up my phone bill by first calling the *Bulletin*'s sister paper in Paris. Why couldn't it be a brother paper? Or are newspapers like ships? And flags? And why are so many inanimate objects referred to as "her" or "she" in the first place? Who makes these decisions? Is there a token male-designated object somewhere out there, other than the old gun-barrel penis symbolism? Did any man stand up and cheer when they started to include us in the naming of hurricanes? And who cares? Even more important, why was my mind even considering such stupid questions?

After three calls, Jane made connections with her friend Mr. Ford at his Paris apartment. Apparently Mr. Ford was not an early riser and didn't much appreciate the call until Jane did a little cooing into his transatlantic ear.

"He'll call us in a few hours," Jane said. "Barney knows someone, who knows someone, supposedly." She looked up at the kitchen clock and smiled. "I don't think it's worth staying up for his call, do you, Nick?"

Indeed I did not. Ford got his wake-up revenge. The

phone next to the bed rang at about four in the morning. I climbed over Jane's back and picked up the receiver, grunting something unintelligible even to me.

"This is the overseas operator. I have a collect call from Paris for Jane Tobin."

"We'll accept," I said, shaking Jane's shoulder and switching on the bed lamp.

She shielded her eyes and swore.

"It's your old boyfriend," I said, handing her the phone. "Collect."

Jane rubbed the sleep from her eyes and took the phone. "Hi, Barney, what's up?"

Me for one. I slipped on my pants and listened to Jane saying mostly, "I see." Then finally, "Barney, would you mind telling all of this to a friend of mine? Nick Polo."

"I'll take it in the office," I said to Jane. I switched on the tape recorder and picked up the phone. "Good morning, Mr. Ford."

"I'll leave you two alone now," Jane said, hanging up.

"Polo, Jane said you wanted some information on a Gene Lembi."

"Right."

"Anything in it for me?"

"Could be, but I'm not sure. If there is, I'll have Jane give it to you."

"Sure, sure," Ford said. "After she's milked the story for all it's worth. You know much about Interpol, Polo?"

"Not as much as I should."

"Okay, let me give you a brief rundown. There are three divisions: The Coordination Division, it manages liaison with police departments throughout the world, takes care of the criminal records system, and goes out with the local gendarmes and helps in kicking in doors and arresting people. The fun stuff. Then there's the Administration Division, which manages their global communications setup. Finally there's the Research Division, which assembles and analyzes all the different reports and tips that come into headquarters. Lembi used to be one of the razzle-dazzle guys in Coordination, until he took a bullet in the leg from a Marseilles gunrunner. Now he's just a glorified clerk in the Research Division. Lembi's on a month's vacation now. That help you?"

"Yes. Thanks. Quite a bit."

"Okay, tell Jane she owes me one."

Jane was snoring lightly when I got back to bed, so I'd have to pass on Ford's message later. I lay there with my hands behind my head, knowing I wasn't going to get back to sleep.

Lembi works out of Interpol's research division. Which would give him access to all the current, and old, files. How did he pick up Claude Martel's name? A report that just came across his desk? A tip about some hot paintings on the gray market? Whatever, once he wanted to stick his nose into Martel's business, he would have access to all of Interpol's records and would also be able to cross-check with the FBI, or even CIA. Lembi had told me himself about Martel's connection with the old OSS. So what the hell was Lembi doing? Playing cowboy on his vacation? Interpol probably pays their people less than good old Uncle Sam pays his. Living in Paris is expensive. According to Lembi, there is a big reward for finding and returning the paintings. But surely an Interpol man couldn't claim the reward himself. If Lembi was playing that game, he'd have to have an accomplice. No problem there. Find the paintings and have someone else turn them in for a split of the reward. Maybe that's what he was pumping me for. Polo the patsy. Lembi would know about my past record. I'd be perfect for him. So would Whitman for that matter. Lembi had checked in with the Alcohol, Tobacco and Firearms office, but hadn't told them he was on vacation. He could use their phone. And their computer, which could run criminal checks. And was no doubt hooked into the city's probation office records, so he could have gotten a line on Lanagan.

Jane rolled over, taking most of the covers with her.

Yes, Lembi looked good. Could he have wired the houseboat with the dynamite? Yes, I'm sure Interpol gave all their agents a good deal of training in explosives.

Was Lanagan already dead when the bomb went off? I had the houseboat staked out for a couple of hours. Was Lanagan inside, with sticks of dynamite protruding out of his vital body orifices, while I was ringing the bell and twisting the doorknob to see if it was locked? I shuddered involuntarily, thinking how close I'd come to getting the final surprise of my life, if that was the case.

Lanagan could have been alive, peeking at me through the upstairs windows. Or he could have come home after I left and hustled back to Claude Martel's house for the handing over of the money to Whitman.

That didn't give the killer much time. I'd gone right back to Islais Creek after leaving Martel's house. The whole round-trip took no more than an hour.

I pulled back some of the blankets and pounded the pillow. It was too convenient. The time period too close. Which meant what? That someone had known that the coast was going to be clear for an hour. Which meant that someone knew that the payoff was on, and maybe even knew that I had been at Islais Creek, but was leaving, to meet with Martel and Whitman, which meant that someone may have planted a bug in Martel's office. That super-duper bug detector on his desk would only check the phone lines. Which meant Michelle Martel. Unless Denise, or Charles the butler, or the cook, or one of the household staff was in on it with someone, which left me back with my three-ring circus of Lembi, Bodine, or Michelle.

I must have dozed off because the sound of the shower running popped my eyes open. It was almost eight. Jane came toddling in with a towel wrapped around her.

"Was Barney Ford helpful?" she asked, taking a comb from her purse and going to work on her hair.

"Very. He says you owe him."

"Right. And you owe me."

"Dinner last night wasn't a big enough payoff?"

"Not nearly," she said, digging through her purse for her mascara and lipstick.

"How about having that chicken you brought last night for breakfast?"

The chicken was a Colonel Sanders reject. We settled for toast and coffee.

The morning *Chronicle*'s story didn't really say much about the explosion at Islais Creek, other than identify both victims, Patrick Lanagan and Roy Whitman. I did get a slight mention: "Police were reportedly interviewing private investigator Nick Polo, who was taking photographs in the area just prior to the explosion."

A companion article went into Whitman's background as a policeman and private investigator.

"I thought you told me you didn't speak to any reporters," Jane protested.

"I didn't. Tehaney must have let out the news on the pictures."

"What's next, Nick?"

"How are you at disguising your voice?" I asked.

We went over her story several times. Even though Chuck Bodine had only heard her speak briefly to Lionel Martel the night of the charity party, I didn't want to give him even the slightest chance of pegging the voice on the phone as Jane's.

She practiced the simple conversation a half dozen times before she was satisfied, finding that simply placing her fingers along the carotid artery on her neck, and speaking through her nose, gave her a voice that would have been at home broadcasting a wrestling match.

I dug through my wallet for the Rolodex card I had typed at Whitman's office, with Bodine's San Francisco address and phone number on it, and passed it to Jane. "Ready?"

She nodded and dialed the number, then made a face, covered the receiver with her hand, and whispered, "Answering machine."

"Leave the message," I whispered back.

She nodded, drummed her fingers on the kitchen wall a few moments, put her hand to her throat, and said, "I saw something at Islais Creek yesterday that I'm sure you're interested in. Meet me at Carmen's Restaurant, at noon today, or I'll peddle my information to the private eye in the newspaper."

"How was I?" Jane asked after hanging up the phone.

"We'll know if he shows up."

♠ ♥ ♣ ♦

This time I was prepared, with my Minolta .35-mm camera with the zoom lens. I was driving Jane's pride and joy convertible. She had parted with it about as easily as Nixon had parted with the tapes. As far as I knew, Bodine hadn't seen my car, but Whitman had, and there was no telling whom he told, and it had been parked around the Martel house more than once, so there was no sense in making myself an easy target. I once ran thirty-four license plates through DMV for an attorney who was sure he was being followed by the feds. His statement at the time was, "Just because I may be paranoid, doesn't mean I'm not really being followed." A little paranoia never hurt anyone, I guess.

I was wearing a battered old dark-blue, porkpie, poplin rain hat and a pair of dark glasses with lenses the size of doughnuts. I set up shop under the freeway at a little after eleven and waited.

Bodine parked his Jaguar sedan a half block from the restaurant at fourteen minutes after twelve. He was alone. He got out of the car, looked around, raised his arms over his head, and stretched. Either he was cramped, or it was a signal of some kind to somebody. I scanned the area. There were too many possibilities: cars, offices, boats, pedestrians.

I clicked away as Bodine walked to the restaurant. He had a sort of jaunty stroll, weaving and bobbing his shoulders as he moved, like a prizefighter getting ready for the bell to ring. Either that or his shorts and shoes were too tight.

I kept the zoom lens on the restaurant's deck, and after a few minutes Bodine wandered out, carrying a beer in his hand. Carmen's was doing a good lunchtime business, and the deck was crowded. Bodine walked up and down the deck's full length twice, moving slowly. Stopping occasionally to take a sip of his beer.

He waited almost half an hour before giving up and exiting the restaurant. Just before he got back into his car, he went into his hands-over-his-head, stretching routine.

I kicked the car's engine over and was a half block behind him when he pulled into the traffic on Third Street. He seemed to be traveling slowly, in no hurry. I kept him in sight and kept swiveling my head back to see if I could spot anyone behind him.

He drove leisurely down Embarcadero. The Bay was a sparkling blue, and the tail end of the noontime joggers were huffing and puffing their way through the businessmen and -women walking reluctantly back to work.

Bodine put the Jag's blinker on a full block before he turned left on Broadway. He slowed for every signal, seemingly a man with all the time in the world. Just before we reached Kearny Street, I spotted a Mercedes in my rearview mirror. A white one. The kind Michelle Martel drove. I pulled over to the curb, turned away from traffic, and picked up one of Jane's maps and tried to look busy. When I glanced around again, Bodine's car was barely visible. The little white Mercedes was only half a block away. I ignored the blaring horns and got back into the traffic flow.

I edged up behind the Merc convertible, and there was

no doubt it was Michelle Martel. She kept pivoting her head left and right. Like me, she was wearing sunglasses, so it was hard to tell if she was making any use of her rearview mirror.

We continued down Broadway. Bodine made an illegal left turn on Powell Street. Michelle was right behind him. I had to wait for a signal change before I could cut in front of the oncoming traffic and play catch-up.

Cable cars clanged down the street, tourists smiling, one hand clutching the handrails, the other their cameras, as the quaint little cars skimmed along the cobbled streets. Cable cars. A tourist's delight, an insurance adjuster's nightmare. Every few months, one of the old beauties would lose its tenuous grip on the underground cable that kept it from being nothing but a Victorian bobsled. People would fall into the streets, under cars, against telephone poles, and the city auditors would groan while waiting for the accident victims' attorneys' calculating phone calls. There would be articles in the papers. A new safety study would be called for. The study would show that it was too expensive to operate the cable system, that the native San Franciscans never really used the cars anymore, that they should be retired. And all the while the cable cars would be clinging and clattering up and down the hills, in as much danger of being replaced as Mickey Mouse was of being banished from Disneyland.

I fumbled with the camera and took a few pictures. Michelle's Merc was almost on Bodine's bumper as our little caravan left Powell for a right turn on Sacramento Street, and then into the garage of a multistory apartment house on Mason Street. I got three good shots as both of their cars disappeared into the building's garage.

28

I parked and debated with myself on what to do next. Wait and see if they hunkered down for the rest of the afternoon, or drop Jane's car back to her and have her make another phone call. I decided to stake out Bodine's place for an hour.

I didn't need nearly that much time. Not more than five minutes after they entered the garage, Michelle Martel's little Merc bolted out of the garage, spinning its wheels as it hit the street.

I followed her for the few minutes it took to get downtown. She pulled into a white zone on Sutter Street, right in front of the sleek glass-and-chrome facade of Martel Galleries, got out of the car, and hurried into the store, almost knocking down a well-dressed couple coming out of the place.

My, my, what had gotten Michelle so riled up?

I drove back to Jane's place, parked her car in the apartment house garage, right next to my rig, and buzzed her doorbell. She came down to let me into the building, first detouring over to the garage and giving her convertible an inspection worthy of a drill sergeant's white-gloving his boot-camp recruits before their first liberty.

"Not a nick or a scratch," I said, transferring the camera to my car.

"How did it go?" she asked as we got into the elevator.

"Bodine showed up, being shadowed by Michelle Martel. They ended up back at Bodine's condo, and Michelle left in a big huff."

"Now what?"

"Get your Actors Guild card ready. It's time for another phone call."

I wrote out a quick script and Jane made her call to Bodine.

"I was there at twelve," she said. "I waited ten minutes. I'll give you one more—"

She winced and pulled the phone away from her ear. I got close enough to hear Bodine's shouting and yelling the kind of encouragement Mike Ditka gives when one of his players drops a sure touchdown pass. She was holding the receiver in two fingers, as if it were a dead mouse she'd just picked up from the floor. I took it out of her hand and broke the connection.

"I think he's mad," I said.

Jane smiled benevolently. "Understatement, Nick. A vanishing art. I'm glad you're reviving it."

♠ ♥ ♣ ♦

The uniformed doorman at Bodine's condo building gave me an appraising look when I asked him to tell Bodine that he had a visitor. He got on the building's intercom.

"Your name, sir?" he asked.

"Nick Polo."

He relayed the information, nodding his head in affirmation. "He says to come right up, sir. Are you a friend of Mr. Bodine's?"

"Not really. Why?"

"He's not in a good mood, sir. Called down earlier and

gave me a good ass-chewing. If you're selling something, I'd pick another day."

Bodine's unit was on the eleventh floor. He was waiting for me when the elevator doors hissed open.

"You son of a bitch," he said, pointing the index finger of his right hand at me as if it were a gun barrel. "You set me up, you no good son of a bitch, didn't you?"

Bodine looked as if he'd had his share of fights along the way, and looked as if he'd won most of them.

I put my hands up in front of me. "Calm down, Bodine. What the hell's the matter with you? I came over to tell you somebody called me on the phone, trying to sell me something, and if I wasn't buying, she was going to sell it to you."

He stared at me, and after a while, some of the fire left his eyes. "What was she selling?"

"Mind if we talk somewhere other than the hallway?" I said.

I followed him down the carpeted hall to an open door. He marched in ahead of me. I could see now the reason for his displeasure. The place had been turned over: paintings off the wall, chairs upturned, a sofa and chair cut open and gutted. I followed him into the kitchen. The pots and pans were scattered along the floor, as were the contents of the freezer and refrigerator. I skirted a container of orange-colored ice cream that was melting and puddling the floor.

"What was she selling?" Bodine asked again.

"She said that she had some information about the explosion at Islais Creek. Said it was for sale, and if I wasn't interested, she'd sell it to you."

"When did you get that call?" he asked, leaning back against the kitchen counter.

"About half an hour ago."

"Bitch," he snapped, bringing his hands together and popping his knuckles. "Called me this morning. Left a message on my machine. Set up a meeting. She didn't show, and when I got back"—he flung his arm out—"this is what I found. Fucking building's supposed to have a full-time security guard. Some asshole walks in here like he owns the building and wrecks my place."

"Any idea how they got in?"

"Hell, no."

"Mind if I look around?"

"Help yourself," he said, stooping down to pick up a large frying pan.

There was a terrace, with an overhanging balcony. I peered over, then up. Someone could have dropped down from the upper balcony, but it would have been a stupid thing to try in broad daylight. There were two entrances. The one I'd come in, and another off the bedroom. There was no evidence of any pry marks around the doors or their frames. They were well-constructed, solid wooden doors, with top-grade locks, which meant that someone hadn't used a credit card or piece of celluloid to jimmy their way in. Which left either a key, or someone who knew how to use a pick.

"Any ideas?" Bodine asked when I got back to the kitchen.

"Looks like whoever got in picked the locks. They're good locks, too. Did you recognize the woman's voice?"

"No," he said. "Come on. Take a listen."

We went into the bedroom, which was more of the same chaos, mattress cut up, dresser drawers open, and clothes thrown around the floor and the bottom of the closet.

"Call must have come in this morning when I was in the shower," Bodine said, punching the button on his answering machine.

Jane's voice sounded startlingly familiar to me, as if her efforts at disguise were wasted. I'd have to have her stay away from Bodine and Michelle Martel.

"Yes, it's the same voice," I told Bodine.

"Sounds like she's trying to disguise it, doesn't it?" he said.

"Hard to say."

He rubbed a hand across his chin. "I remember playing poker with you, Polo. You were good at bluffing. Damn good. How do I know you're not bluffing now? That you didn't set this whole thing up?"

"What for? I don't know why the woman even called me, except my name was in the newspaper story on the bombing. Why did she call you?"

He shook his head. "No. I'll pass this hand." The fire was coming back to his eyes. "Get out of here. Now."

"I spoke to the cops after the explosion, Bodine. They're sure dynamite was used. Did you use much dynamite in your days on the oil rigs?"

He reached for a large chef's knife on the counter. "You're watching the wrong movies, Polo. We never used dynamite, just nitro." He waved the knife in my direction. "And the way my hands shake nowadays, I'd be crazy to fool with anything that dangerous."

"I know that Roy Whitman got you and Lionel out of that mess with the underage prostitutes. What else was Whitman doing for you? The police are going to find your name on his office address Rolodex."

"Get the fuck out of here," Bodine said, coming toward me. The hand holding the knife looked anything but shaky, and I beat a hasty retreat to the elevator.

"Don't expect a Christmas bonus this year," I told the doorman as I headed back for my car.

I went back to my flat and called Jane and filled her in on Bodine's apartment's being ransacked.

"No wonder he was so mad when I called him the second time," she said.

"Yes, and he looks like the kind of guy who stays mad for a long time. Have you got anything on for tonight?"

"Well, Tony had asked me out to dinner."

"Tony? The guy who drove you to the hospital from the party?"

"Yes, but if you—"

"No, no. Keep your date. It's better that we're not seen together right away. No telling what Bodine will do. He may have someone watching me."

"You really think he's involved now, Nick?"

"I don't know. But let's play it safe for a while. I'll call you in the morning."

I walked down to Mrs. Damonte's flat. She gave me one of her rare smiles. Of course the two twenty-dollar bills I was placing in her hand may have had something to do with it.

"Why don't you go out tonight, Mrs. Damonte? Have dinner. See a movie."

She took an old-fashioned coin purse from her dress pocket. I expected to see moths fly out from the inside of her purse and suddenly grow into the size of the pterodactyls in Japanese horror movies, but there wasn't even a visible puff of dust. She dropped in the two twenties and put the purse back in her pocket.

"You want me away from here? How long?"

"Oh, nine or ten o'clock ought to do it."

"I may be later. Let's have drink."

This had turned into a banner occasion. Usually she only offers me a drink when she wants me to paint, repair, or replace something or meet one of her nieces.

She took a bottle of Rock And Rye from her kitchen cabinet, put about two shots apiece into small, delicately stemmed wineglasses, gulped hers in about three swallows, and waited while I finished trying to sip the sweetish liquor down without gagging.

When I got back to my place, I rinsed my mouth out with a decent bourbon, put a pot of coffee on, and made some tuna sandwiches. When the coffee was done, I poured a cup, put the rest in a thermos, turned on the answering machine, loosened the revolver in its holster on my hip, got a flashlight from a kitchen drawer, made sure all the lights were off, and waited.

I heard Mrs. Damonte's front door close a little after five. I worked my way slowly through the coffee and sandwiches, wondering which way he'd come in. If he did come.

Even though my front door was pretty well shut off from view from the street, I was betting on the back door. There's something about the back door that always seems safer. Besides, for some reason, most people seem to put a much better lock on their front door than the back one.

The phone rang four times. The first call was from Bob Tehaney. He left a message on my answering machine, asking me to call him. That was a little after six-thirty. There was a call at just after eight. Another a few minutes later, and still another a few minutes after that. No messages. Just a quick hangup as soon as the answering machine's message clicked on.

The last call must have been from somewhere real close by, because within a couple of minutes there were footsteps coming up the front steps. Then the doorbell rang. It looked as if I had lost my bet. He was coming in the front way. Either he was lazy or very confident. I waited. He played with the doorbell again, then got to work.

He was good. Very good. A lot faster than I would have been. Once the lock was turned, he opened the door quickly and stepped inside. A pencil-thin flashlight beam started playing along the floor.

I held my arm way out to the left and flicked on my flashlight and said, "Freeze, or I'll kill you where you stand, Mr. Lembi."

"*Merde*," was his only response.

I flicked on the light switch with an elbow and pocketed the flashlight.

He was one of your better-dressed burglars. Another well-cut suit; beige this time. "You know the drill," I told him, waving him away from the door with the gun. "On your knees. Empty your pockets. Slowly. Just use one hand. Turn the pockets inside out."

"Surely you wouldn't use that gun, Mr. Polo. Shooting an Interpol agent would not be very wise."

"The first bullet would go right into your good leg, Lembi. That would give you a matching pair."

"Ah, you've been doing some checking, haven't you?"

"Funny way for a man to spend his vacation, breaking and entering. Find anything interesting at Bodine's place?"

He got down awkwardly on one knee and began taking things out of his pockets: keys, two wallets, handkerchiefs, some coins, and a zippered black leather pouch.

"That's all of it," he said.

"Lie down flat. Arms spread out."

I patted him down from behind, sticking the gun in the base of his skull. He was clean. No gun, no knife, no saps. I kicked the zippered leather pouch across the floor, then walked over and picked it up. It was a set of picks and tension wrenches, thirty-four in all. I knew burglars who would have sold their grandmothers for that kind of equipment.

"May I get up now?" Lembi said from the floor.

"Not until we talk. And if I don't like what I hear, I'm calling the local police. Interpol or not, you'll have a lot of explaining to do."

He rolled over on his back and put his arms behind his head. "You seem to have the drop on me. Isn't that what you Americans say?"

"Some of us. Quit stalling. Why did you break into Bodine's place, and why did you come here?"

"This is embarrassing enough. But if you were recording this . . ." He gave his shoulders a shrug.

"No recorders. You'll have to take my word for it. But believe me, I wasn't kidding about calling the cops. Now talk."

"It would be more comfortable if I could sit."

I had no idea what type of tricks they taught the boys at

Interpol, and I wasn't about to give him a chance to display them. "Tough it out, Lembi."

"All right. The story I told you about the missing paintings, confiscated by the Germans, was all true. And there is no doubt that Claude Martel came away with some of the prize pieces after the war.

"Vincent van Gogh came to Arles in 1888, a small town in the south of France, on the Rhône River, some fifty miles from Marseilles. He stayed for over a year and completed over two hundred oils, and half as many watercolors. One of van Gogh's favorite subjects was sunflowers. He painted them in full bloom, alone, in a vase, even as dried seed heads. His fellow artist, Paul Gauguin, had such admiration for the works that he himself did a canvas he titled *Van Gogh Painting Sunflowers*. One of the van Gogh sunflower series recently sold for 39.9 million dollars. Not as much as his work entitled *Irises* received, 53.9 million dollars, but truly an amazing sum. The megamillionaires have run the prices up so high that no museum can afford them anymore.

"One particular van Gogh sunflower painting belonged to my grandparents. They lost everything when the Nazis threw them on the train. My father survived the war. He used to tell me stories about the painting. How my grandparents loved it. I looked for it. Checked reports, interviewed dealers. There were rumors that it had disappeared to Russia, to South America with Mengele. That it was destroyed in a bombing raid by the Allies. Then, about a year ago, a report came that it was coming on the market. From America. I checked all the available sources. They led to one man. Claude Martel. The painting was too famous to show in the open market, of course. Whoever did buy it would have to be the kind of a man who would keep it for himself, for his lifetime, maybe even his children's lifetime. It is worth millions now. Think of what it will be worth in twenty, fifty, even a hundred years from now."

His face showed pain, and he wiggled his back into the

carpet. I wasn't buying it. "Go on," I said. "Sounds good so far."

"As quick as the stories about the painting surfaced, they stopped. The painting was suddenly 'not available.' Then, Martel popped up in Europe, and as I told you before, works that the Nazis had captured began circulating. As did rumors of the van Gogh. One man, a dealer in Paris, told me he actually made a bid for it. Twenty-two million dollars. For a painting that could not even be shown in public! Do you believe it, Mr. Polo? Twenty-two million. And the offer was turned down! There had been a better offer. I squeezed this dealer, as well as every contact I had. The story was this. That the painting was going to Japan. The price? No set price, really. It was part of a business deal. A piece of the negotiations. Clever, eh? That way Martel didn't even have to worry about laundering all the money he'd be making by getting rid of it. Just a negotiated business deal. But the price would be millions and millions of dollars less than it should have been. Who would be the wiser? I knew if the painting went to Japan, I'd never see it again. I was ready to confront Martel in Paris. Scare him, maybe kill him if necessary. But that was when he got news of the robbery and bolted home."

"What made you think that Bodine or I had the damn thing?"

He smiled knowingly. "Whitman has Bodine's name on his desk address thing"—he rolled his hand in the air—"what do you call them?"

"Rolodex. So you broke into Whitman's office. When was that?"

"Right after you. Thanks for leaving the iron gate open for me. I got into the office next door. The electrician's. I could hear you moving around. Using the typewriter. After you left, I went into Whitman's office. I was puzzled at first about your using the typewriter. Then I found Bodine's card on that address thing. You made a copy, didn't you?"

"Did you get into his safe?" I said.

"My friend, those picks are good. But not for a safe."

"What makes you think your grandparents' painting wasn't blown up in the explosion at the houseboat?"

"It wasn't an accidental explosion, and no one would be stupid enough to blow up something like that."

I holstered my gun. "Get up, Lembi. Look around if you like. But don't make a mess like you did at Bodine's place."

29

Gene Lembi struggled to his feet. "I don't think a search will be necessary. But I could use a drink."

"What do you want?"

"Anything."

I started another pot of coffee, then put a glass and a bottle of Christian Brothers brandy on the kitchen table. "Help yourself," I told Lembi.

He sat down and massaged his left knee. "Who do you think has the painting now?"

"I haven't a clue."

He poured himself some of the brandy. "I think it's someone named Martel. And I think if I don't find it within the next couple of days, it will be gone forever."

"There is more than one Martel. You can cross Claude off the list. He certainly wouldn't have any reason to steal the paintings from himself."

"Maybe, maybe not," Lembi said, staring into his glass of brandy. "He could have set up the whole operation. Maybe he heard someone was after him." He looked up at me. "You've been in his house. The painting could be there now."

I considered it for a minute. "No. If he wanted to do that, there would have been a lot of easier ways to handle it."

"Then there is Lionel," Lembi said.

"Would he cut off a piece of his own finger? No. I doubt it. Besides, Lionel doesn't look like the kind of guy who would take that big a gamble."

The coffee had finished perking. I poured two cups and placed one in front of him. "I'm surprised you haven't broken into Lionel's apartment."

"I'd like to." He dumped the remains of the brandy into his coffee. "Lionel interests me. We only have his word that the paintings were taken that night. He could have taken them himself earlier that day. Or simply moved them somewhere in the Martel house. They could still be there. Exactly how many paintings did Claude Martel tell you were stolen?"

"Three."

"Three paintings. In frames they would be cumbersome. Someone would have noticed their being carried out of the house that night."

There was something else Lembi didn't know. That the paintings were all neatly wrapped and ready for transport. Or at least he wasn't letting on that he knew. "You're forgetting that Roy Whitman was in charge of security."

"Why Whitman? Why hire someone like him in the first place?" Lembi said.

Ah, so he didn't know about the lollypop whorehouse connection, either. "What's your case on the rest of the Martels? Denise and Michelle?"

He blew on the coffee to cool it down, then took a deep sip. "I don't think Denise is involved. She's just a nice, fun-loving woman who married an old bastard for his money. I don't think she knows anything of Claude's business interests."

"You sound like you've had personal contact with Mrs. Martel."

"I bumped into her in Paris."

That must have been an interesting bump. "Then that leaves Michelle."

"Yes," he agreed. "It does. She is the one with the true Claude Martel genes in her makeup."

"And she has all the contacts with the art world."

"Yes, that is my big fear. If it is Michelle, the paintings are probably sold already." He stood and put out his hand. "I'm sorry for the trouble tonight."

"Tell me something. Professional curiosity. How did you get into Bodine's building?"

He started limping toward the front door. "Distraction. Some firecrackers in the street. The doorman couldn't resist venturing out to see what was going on. I slipped inside. The rest was easy. Remember the reward, Mr. Polo. I would be very generous."

I watched Lembi until he was all the way down the stairs. Reward. What if I did stumble across the paintings? Who the hell would I turn them over to? The police? If they got their hands on them, what would they do with them? Lembi acted as if he were only interested in the van Gogh that supposedly belonged to his grandparents. Even if he was telling the truth, could he really put in a claim of ownership after all these years? If Martel got the paintings back, they'd go back into hibernation in his vault just long enough for him to find the right buyer.

Questions, questions, Polo. Get some answers.

It was a little late to go calling on people in person, so I used the phone. The number Inspector Tehaney left on my answering machine was the one at the Homicide Bureau. He'd be long gone by now, and if it was anything really important, he'd have tried getting ahold of me again.

I tried Lionel Martel's number, but there was no answer.

I called Claude Martel's house. Good old Charles answered the phone. He informed me that Mr. Martel was out.

"Is Michelle in?"

"No, sir, she is not."

"How about Mrs. Martel?"

If Charles had a sense of humor he would have responded, "Yeah, how about Mrs. Martel?" Instead he said, "I'll connect you, sir."

It took a minute or two.

"Nick," she said when she came on the line. "I was wondering when you'd call."

"Busy, busy. Is it too late for you to slip out for a drink?"

"Oh, my. I wish you would have called a half hour ago. Now I'm all ready for bed. I don't have anything on, including my makeup."

"You don't really need makeup, Denise."

"Oh, my, I do love that kind of talk. Why don't you stop by here for a nightcap?"

"No, not a good idea. Claude wouldn't like it."

"He's not here. He left this afternoon and didn't come back for dinner. Come on. Stop by. Just one drink."

"All right. But just one drink. There's a couple of questions I'd like to ask you?"

Denise giggled. "Let's be exact. Like they do in the spy movies. We'll synchronize our watches. You be here in exactly thirty minutes. That way I can be at the front door, and we won't have to bother Charles."

"Make it forty minutes and you've got a date."

I drove by the Martel Galleries on Sutter Street first. There was no sight of Michelle's car, but there was a stately dark-brown Rolls-Royce, parked right in front. The streets were almost deserted. The gallery lights were on. I got out of the car and peered in. There were groups of statues and massive canvases pinpointed by track lighting. I could see some shadows moving in the back of the building. Was Michelle working late? What better place to hide a painting than in a gallery? I waited a few minutes, but got nothing for my trouble other than cold feet.

I parked in front of a fire hydrant a block away from the Martel house and at the appointed time, knocked softly on the front door.

It sprang open immediately. Denise's long locks were piled up on top of her head. She was all giggles and jiggles in a demure black robe, buttoned from the bottom right up to her chin. She put her index finger in front of her lips, made a *ssshhhh* sound, then grabbed my arm and tugged me upstairs.

"Wait," I said. "I just saw a car drive around the block. What does Claude drive?"

"A Rolls, darling."

"What color?"

"As brown as the hair on your head," she murmured. "Now come with me."

When we were on the second floor, I disengaged my hand and in a voice a little above a whisper, said, "Denise, where's Claude's room?"

"Down the end of the hall, darling." She grabbed my hand again.

"And where's Michelle's room?"

She arched an eyebrow. "Whatever do you want to know that for, Nicky?"

"So I can avoid it."

"Hmmm." She pointed a long red nail down the hall. "That one," she said. "Now, come inside."

Under the demure robe was a sheer, black teddy with a lace V-front. She had on black stockings, the kind that don't need a garter to hold them up. A bottle of opened champagne and two glasses sat on a tray alongside the bed.

She poured two glasses of the wine and stood holding them in a provocative pose. "Thirsty, or . . . ?"

Or came first. Then the wine, most of which she consumed. I questioned her about her European trip with Claude. After all, it was the real purpose of my visit, wasn't it? Right? Right. Anyway, I did question her about it. She gave me a tourist's view of the sights and shopping bargains.

"What about Claude? Doesn't he like to shop?" I asked.

177

"Just at those dreary old art galleries, darling. Unless it's a big opening with a party, I try to avoid those."

"So you had some time on your own. That must have been fun. Did you happen to run into a man named Gene Lembi while you were there?"

The little-girl smile turned into a grimace. "Why do you ask such a question?"

"It's about the job I'm doing for Claude. I think a man may have been following you and Claude while you were in Europe." I gave her a description of Lembi.

Her hand went to her face when I mentioned his stiff-leg limp.

"Gene. Yes, but he said his name was Montand, you know, like the actor."

"So you did meet him?"

"Briefly. But I didn't tell him anything about Claude. What could I tell him?"

"What did he ask you?"

"Nothing, nothing, we just talked. Briefly.

"Nicky, my husband puts up with certain things because he is realistic. He is much more French than American when it comes to sex. Much more. There are times when he can't participate with me, but likes to watch me. With other men. Do you understand? But if he ever found out that I was telling a rival about his business affairs, that would be the end of me. When we married, I signed a prenuptial agreement. If he leaves me, I would wind up with nothing. I would never do anything that foolish."

I topped off her glass. "What about Roy Whitman? Did you ever have any—conversations with him?"

"Never." She looked down into her glass, watching the bubbles tumble to the surface. Her face broke into a reluctant smile. "I think that Michelle beat me to Mr. Whitman."

"They were friendly?"

"I think so. I saw them talking. He had that look of interest on his face, and once I saw him leaving her room."

"In the last few days?"

"Yes. Why?"

"No real reason. Who else is Michelle interested in? Besides you."

She sat up. "I swear, Nicky, the night with you was the first time that ever happened."

She looked me right in the eyes when she said it. I almost believed her. "What about Michelle and other men? Chuck Bodine for instance."

She tilted her head back and laughed. "Chuck? Why he's much too old for her, darling, I . . ." The silliness of the statement hit her and she laughed so hard she spilled her wine all over herself.

"Too old. I am the one to talk, eh? But I never thought of Chuck and Michelle together. They just don't seem right for each other."

She handed me her empty glass and ran the palms of her hands down her throat and breasts, then put her champagne-damp hands behind my head and pulled me to her.

♠ ♥ ♣ ♦

It was after one o'clock when I heard someone walking down the hallway. Then there was the sound of a door slamming.

Denise woke up. "Claude," she said with a yawn. "He always slams doors when he's in a bad mood." She patted the mattress. "Come back to bed." She turned over and drifted right back to sleep.

I got into my clothes and slipped out the door. The hallway was empty. There was enough lighting so you could see your way. I went down to the door Denise had pointed out as being to Michelle's room. I put my ear to the door and couldn't hear anything, then dropped to the rug. There was no sign of any lights from inside the room. I tried the handle. Surprise, surprise, it was unlocked. I opened the door centimeter by centimeter. No sound at all from inside the room. I went inside and closed the door behind me, standing there motionless while I waited for my eyes to adjust to the darkness. I edged inside the room and could make out the bed. The white satin bedspread was smooth and unruffled.

I turned on the light next to the bedstand. The room was done in Louis XVI, or XV, anyway, a Louis who liked his furniture painted gray with carved and gilded decorations. I gave the room a quick toss, peeking into drawers and closets, not really finding out much, except that Michelle spent a lot of money on clothes and makeup. There was only one painting in the room, that of an overweight woman in a low-cut, red ball gown. She looked as if she was waiting for someone to ask her to dance, and it was going to be a long wait.

Michelle was too smart a girl to hide a painting under the bed, but I got down on all fours and peeked anyway. Nothing. Not even a dust ball. I exited the room wondering where Michelle was spending the night. As I started down the steps, I heard the sound of the front door opening. I ducked back into Denise's room, left the door open a crack, and watched as Michelle Martel came bouncing down the hallway. The look on her face would have discouraged a trained attack dog from approaching her. She went right to her room, slamming the door after her. Maybe slamming doors was a Martel tradition. I made sure I closed the front door as quietly as possible on my way out.

30

Inspector Bob Tehaney's call woke me up the next morning.

"I got your message last night, Bob," I told him. "I was going to call you in a little while."

"The message last night wasn't very important. This morning's is. I'll be by in a few minutes. Be ready. We're talking a ride down to the airport."

His horn beeped some twenty minutes later. I went down to meet him carrying my morning cup of coffee.

"What's the big rush?" I asked, climbing into his unmarked car, which was so dirty and beat-up it made mine resemble Claude Martel's Rolls in comparison.

Tehaney pulled away in a jerk, causing some of my coffee to slop over onto my lap. Great way to start a morning.

Tehaney got a Lucky Strike going, then said, "Yesterday I went to see this Charles Bodine you told me about. He wasn't in. The doorman said you had been by to see Bodine. I got inside his place. It was a mess. I called him later last night, he still wasn't around." He put the car's red light on, pushed the siren button, swerved around a double-parked truck and a slow-moving line of cars, into the oncoming traffic lane, then made a hard right onto the freeway ramp.

"Got a call from San Mateo sheriff's office down at the airport garage. Some kids tried to break into a green Jaguar sedan. Got more than they bargained for. There's a body in the trunk. Car's license shows it's owned by a Mr. Charles Bodine."

The San Francisco International Airport is located thirteen miles south of the city, in neighboring San Mateo County. The body, therefore, would fall into the San Mateo sheriff's jurisdiction, something I'm sure pleased Tehaney more than a little bit, because with jurisdiction came most of the work. If the body in the car's trunk was Bodine, then the tie-in between his death and those of Whitman and Lanagan would be pretty obvious, drawing Tehaney into the investigation, but the drudgery of the initial investigation, and the physical handling of the evidence, would all be San Mateo's.

It was Bodine all right. He was curled up on his right side in the trunk of the Jaguar. His head was tilted up to the left at an unnatural angle. His eyes were rolled up into the back of his head, and there was a gaping wound under his neck.

The average human body holds from ten to twelve pints of blood, equal to about one-thirteenth of the body's total weight. The majority of Bodine's was lying under him in a thickening mass.

I pulled my eyes away.

Tehaney asked, "That him?"

"That's him, Bob."

There was the usual crowd standing around: a few uniformed cops, paramedics, two guys in business suits who had something to do with running the airport, and the dozen or so ghouls that seem to congregate at any disaster scene.

I walked away and leaned on a cement post. Twenty minutes later Tehaney joined me, an unlit cigarette dangling from his lips.

"San Mateo coroner is going to handle the body. I'm

182

going to be stuck around here for a while. Want to hang around?"

"No, I'll get a cab back to town."

The county crime-lab wagon pulled up alongside the Jaguar, bringing another crowd of ghouls to gawk at the proceedings.

"When did you see him last?" said Tehaney.

"Yesterday afternoon. At his place. You can check with the doorman."

"Any idea of where he went after you saw him?"

"No. He was mad. Mad as hell at whoever broke into his place."

"Yeah. Whoever." Tehaney must have forgotten about the unlit butt already in his mouth. He shook another cigarette out of its pack and had it headed for his mouth when he discovered the other one.

"Shit," he said. "And I thought the legs were the first thing to go. Keep in touch, Nick. I'll want to talk to you later."

The cabdriver tried to get a line of chatter going on the drive back to San Francisco, but my grunted replies finally gave him the hint I wasn't in a gabby mood. I had him drop me back at my flat.

I had skipped breakfast, and after viewing the mortal remains of Charles Bodine, I felt I would probably get along without lunch and dinner, too. I made a pot of coffee, more out of habit than desire, and sat at the kitchen table watching it brew.

I called Jane Tobin, catching her at the *Bulletin*, and told her about the Bodine murder. The story would be fair game; the newspapers and TV-radio people always had someone monitoring the police radio waves. I didn't think Tehaney would appreciate my letting the Martel family in on the news. That was a chore he was welcome to.

Charles Bodine: big, rough, tough Texan. Gutted like a steer. It would be interesting to see what the coroner turned up. He'd have a tough job determining the time of death. The temperature at the airport at night is always chilly, and the garage is open to the night air, so the body's temperature would have stayed quite low, warming up a little only when the sun came up in the morning. Even under ideal conditions—with the victim's body in a closed room, with a steady temperature—the coroner would have a tough time pinning time of death to any closer than five or six hours.

I couldn't see Bodine dying without putting up a fight. My lists of suspects didn't exactly look like a group that could overpower him: Claude Martel was in good shape—I knew that from his handshake—but he was not only smaller, he was a good fifteen or more years older than Bodine. Michelle may be lean and hard, but Bodine could have dealt with her easily with one hand. And speaking of one hand, that's exactly what Lionel Martel had right now, so another mismatch. As for Denise Martel, again a physical mismatch, and besides, what motive could she have?

Of course any one of them could have hired someone to do the job. Or it could be one of those coincidence things. Bodine was the kind of man who would make a lot of enemies over his lifetime.

But if it wasn't a hired killer, then either Bodine was caught completely off guard, or he knew his killer and had gotten careless.

Or, of course, there was Mr. Interpol, Gene Lembi. He was strong enough to take Bodine on and win. A lot would depend on the time of death. I had heard Claude come into the Martel house, and I saw Michelle and Denise there after one in the morning. It's true that one or all could have left the house right after I did, so all that really proved nothing.

The killer got a bad break in that the cops stumbled upon Bodine's body so quickly. Normally a car could sit in the airport parking garage for weeks before the police took particular notice of it. The terrible odors that would come out of the trunk might bring them into it sooner, but the killer, he or she, could have counted on at least a week.

Still, the airport parking lot pointed to an amateur. The airport garage is far too busy a place to attempt a murder. Bodine must have been killed somewhere else, then taken down to the airport. That would have been a nervous drive. There was always the possibility of getting into an accident, or of the car's breaking down. Remote, but enough to give Mr. or Ms. Murderer a real nervous stomach during the trip.

Once in the garage, then what? The killer had to get back home. The obvious choice was a taxi. But then he—or she—would have to worry about being remembered by the cabdriver. The cabbies at the airport have to have a county permit to make their pickups, so it was possible for the police to check with each and every one of them, show each driver a picture of a suspect, ask if they remembered driving the person. Possible, but improbable. Just finding all the drivers would be a long, difficult task, and unless the fare was a very big, or very small, tipper, they never remember them. Still, it was something for Bodine's killer to think about. So what would you do? You're at the airport. Why not a short flight? Hell, they even had flights just across the Bay to Oakland. I'd pick something a little farther away though. Flights to Los Angeles take off every half hour. So you jet down to L.A., then make a quick turnaround, but not back to San Francisco. Make it Oakland. Then a half-hour cab ride across the Bay Bridge and back to San Francisco. Turnaround time could be as little as five hours. Nice scenario, but only if the killer is acting alone. What if there was an accomplice? Then they would have driven down in two cars. Dropped off the Jag, and gone back to wherever they came from. Or it could have been a pro. A lazy professional who was paid for the job and just dropped the body at the airport and took a long flight home.

I poured myself a cup of the coffee and sat there drinking and kicking ideas around, getting nothing for it other than a headache and a sour taste in my mouth.

The jangling of the phone brought me out of my reverie. It was Gene Lembi.

"I just heard the news. They found Charles Bodine's body in the trunk of a car at the airport," he said.

"I know. I'm the one who IDed the corpse."

"Why you?"

"Bob Tehaney picked me for the job. He knew I could identify him."

"How was he killed? Shot?"

"No. His throat was slashed."

"Another knife," Lembi said.

My brain was not up to his normal subspeed. "Another knife?"

"Yes. They used a knife to slice off Lionel Martel's fingertip."

"That's stretching a connection, Lembi. Tehaney will probably want to talk to you about this."

"Why me?" he said in an accusing tone. "Did you tell him about last night?"

"No. Not yet."

"Even if you did, Polo, it would be my word against yours."

"Except that maybe I did have a tape recorder going during your true confessions act. Keep in touch," I said before hanging up. For some reason making Lembi sweat gave me a feeling of pleasure.

My stomach had always been stronger than my brain, and it overpowered any lingering memories of the vision of Bodine's body and ordered me to get it something to eat. I whipped up a cheese omelet and thought about what Gene Lembi had said about the knives. I'd have bet money that Pat Lanagan had been the one who cut off Lionel's finger. And Lanagan was blown apart in the explosion. His rap sheet showed he was a longtime breaking-and-entry man.

There were no armed robberies listed. Or assault and batteries. Once a crook learns a trade, he usually sticks to it. But anyone could use a knife. Couldn't they?

♠   ♥   ♣   ♦

They treat you like a criminal. Mentally retarded, low-life criminal. Even if you're the good guy. Even if you've got a badge in your pocket that shows you're a policeman. They are not the same ones who say falling in love is wonderful; no, they are the guys in the shiny blue jackets with the fake-fur collars and the baseball-style caps that say SAN QUENTIN on the front.

The state prison was gray. The weather was gray. The little office just inside the gates was gray, except for some faded green linoleum. You stand behind a counter, the top half screened with thick wire. They make you shove all your possessions in a metal box, then they run a hand-held metal detector up and down your body. Then you wait with the other visitors, mostly wives and children of convicts, while the guards keep a smug look on their faces and make inside jokes, then stare at you and dare you to laugh.

Eventually a battered bus—gray, what else?—picks you up and drives you deeper into the compound. You get out and go into a waiting room. More gray, the floors a checkerboard of black and white tiles, more chipped than not. One wall is taken up with nothing but vending machines, selling everything from coffee to Coke to sandwiches to soup to fruit to candy. The coffee and candy machines seem to be the only ones doing any business. Every few minutes an inmate will come through a heavy metal door with a guard. These are the trusties, the ones with visiting privileges. They look cold and sullen, even after they kiss the ladies and hug the kids.

I waited. Eventually a short, thin man in a dark-brown

suit carrying a thick manila folder came over and asked for "Mr. Polo."

"That's me."

He told me his name was Morgan, then led me into an anteroom with thick glass windows, so smudged from fingerprints on both sides you could barely see through them. There was an oak table, the top discolored from years of sweating palms, and two wooden chairs bolted to the ground.

"Inspector Paulsen told us to cooperate with you. I'll have to stay here while you look at the file. If you need anything copied, I'll see what I can do, as long as it's not confidential."

I thanked him and started picking my way through Patrick Lanagan's prison record. It didn't take long. After fifteen minutes I handed him back the file. "I'd like to talk to the prison doctor, Mr. Morgan."

His smooth face accordioned in troubled wrinkles.

"I don't know if that is possible." He looked at his wristwatch. "I didn't realize you'd want to interview anyone, and the doctor is always very busy, so we may have to schedule another appointment."

"Look," I told him. "If I slipped and fell, bumped my head, or cut myself, I'd have to see him right away, right?"

He grudgingly admitted the truth of that statement, so I pressed on. "All I want to do is talk to him about the former prisoner Lanagan. Won't take more than two minutes. We can even do it on the phone."

The phone conversation with the prison doctor actually took a little over five minutes. I thanked Mr. Morgan for all his extra efforts.

"No problem. The bus will be back in ten or so minutes, to take you back to the parking lot."

It was closer to forty minutes, which is about as long as I ever want to be in prison again, even in the visitors' waiting room. The smells and the air of despair sink in right through your clothes and into your pores. I had served six months in Lompoc penitentiary, which was like a country club compared to San Quentin, but I still woke up sweating in the middle of the night, grateful as hell when I found out I was home, in my own bed, and not in the old crossbar hotel.

When I finally got out of there and back to my car, my first inclination was to drive home and take a long, hot shower, but I had one more stop to make.

♠   ♥   ♣   ♦

It was my day for doctor visits. I parked in a doctor's-only designated spot in the lot at Mt. Zion Hospital, then flashed the old buzzer again and told the nurse, "I just want to see him for a minute,"

"Dr. Chung is very busy, Inspector. You should have called and let us know you were coming."

She was one of the stern, efficient-looking angels of mercy, her uniform all starched and snowy white, her hair done up in a bun and covered by one of those silly hats they have to wear. The plastic nameplate over her left breast showed she was KOWALSKI, R.N.

I gave her a sincere smile, because if ever there was an underpaid, underappreciated group of people, it's nurses. How they can put up with emptying bedpans, bandaging and unbandaging infectious wounds, watching their patients die in front of them, and dodging ass-pinching doctors is beyond me. God bless each and every one of them. "I apologize for not calling, but if you can slip me in to see him, I'd greatly appreciate it."

She told me to wait in the waiting room. I'd had enough of those for the day. Besides, while not considering myself a hypochondriac, I did find that if I spent more than a few minutes in a hospital waiting room, I suddenly developed a running nose, sore throat, and an itch in places were it was embarrassing to scratch in public. I prowled up and down the hall, stopping at an ever-present vending machine. I'd had more than my share of caffeine for the day, so I tried a cup of what was advertised on the machine as "hot chocolate." They were half right. It was hot.

Nurse Kowalski spotted me and waved me back to Dr. Chung's office.

Chung was in his forties, with shiny black hair and patient black eyes behind wireless-rimmed glasses.

I explained my needs.

"Oh, yes," he said. "I remember the case. It went very well. The patient was cooperative. Not in much pain at all. The cut was clean, almost surgical, and the paramedics had done an excellent job in transporting the severed fingertip in ice. A good job all around. I fully expect the finger to be as good as new, once the healing process is completed. Are there complications?"

"No. Not from your end, Doctor."

I went back to my flat and called Claude Martel and told him I wanted to stop by his place. "Why don't you make it a family affair. Have everyone there for dinner, again."

"I suppose there is a purpose behind all this, Mr. Polo?"

"Yes. I think I'll have some good news, and some bad news for you. I'll be over at seven."

I'd just hung up when the phone rang again.

"Coroner can't pin the time of death any closer than between six last night and six this morning," Inspector Robert Tehaney told me. "The doorman at Bodine's building saw him at six-thirty last night. Bodine had called in some people to clean up his place, and he told the doorman to make sure they didn't walk away with anything valuable. Then Bodine took off in his Jaguar."

"Nothing after that?"

"Not that I know of. What about you?"

"The last time I saw him was yesterday afternoon, Bob."

"That's not what I mean, Polo. You holding out on me on this?"

"I don't know of anyone who saw Bodine after I did,

Bob. I can tell you this, if it'll help. Claude Martel's Rolls-Royce was parked in front of the Martel Gallery on Sutter Street, around nine-thirty last night. At ten o'clock Denise Martel was home. Had been for some time. Both Claude and Michelle Martel came into the house shortly after one A.M.

"How the hell do you know all of this, Nick?"

"I was working for Claude Martel on the recovery of his paintings, remember?"

"And does your work include baby-sitting his wife and watching when he comes home?"

"A man's got to do what a man's got to do, Bob. Anything good come from the crime lab or the coroner?"

"Nah. Not really. Bodine was stabbed all right. Several times in the back, penetration made deep, all the way through to the heart. That was probably enough to finish him off. The cut across the throat made it positive."

"Anything else new, Bob?"

"Well, I heard from Donnie Hansen. He's sure the houseboat was blown with dynamite. He said there was a burglary, at Bogios Explosives down in San Bruno last week. Not much taken; one box of dynamite, some blasting caps, some office equipment. Secretary's desk was rifled and a portable TV and radio are missing, too, but you know those burglaries; the victim always pads the list. But Donnie is pretty sure it's the same dynamite."

Either the victim padded the list, or the burglar was someone who went in for something special, such as the dynamite, and couldn't resist seeing what else was available. It fit the picture in my mind of how Pat Lanagan would handle a job.

"Gene Lembi called me about the murder," I said. "Told me he heard about it on the radio."

"Lembi? The Interpol guy?"

"Right."

"What's his interest in Bodine?"

"You might ask him."

"I might ask a lot of people a lot more questions, including you, Nick. Don't go away on any long trips."

A long trip was just what I needed. I settled for the short drive out to Pacific Heights.

Claude Martel was in his customary position, sitting behind his desk, cigar in hand. The hand was visibly shaking. He looked old and worn. Another week like this last one and he'd be joining Chuck Bodine in that great art gallery in the sky.

"You heard about Bodine, I guess," he said.

"Yes. I sure did. I'd like to see the inside of the vault once more, Mr. Martel."

"For what purpose?"

"For the purpose of finding out just where your paintings are right now."

That certainly caught his interest. He got up to his feet and went over to the vault, making sure I wasn't within peeking distance as he dialed the combination.

It looked just as it did on my last visit. Neat, clean. Martel must have done his own vacuuming and dusting in there. No household help allowed. I went over to the wall where the safety-deposit-type boxes were. There were a total of thirty-six of them, all neatly numbered.

"Does each of these have a separate key?" I asked Martel.

"No. One key fits all the boxes."

"Did you check out each box after the paintings were stolen?"

"Yes. Certainly. Nothing was missing."

"Is there a special box where you keep your very important papers: wills, the documents related to what will happen to Martel, Inc. when you die, things like that?"

"Will? What the hell does my will have to do with this?"

"Maybe nothing. But is it in one of these?"

He nodded his head several times, as a bull does before

he gets ready to charge. "There's no reason for you to see my will, Polo. What the hell are you trying to prove?"

"Which box?"

We stared at each other for a good minute, then he walked over and tapped his finger on box number seven.

It was one of the larger-sized boxes, right at eye level, which made it easy.

"Let me guess," I told Martel. "There's one key, and you have it with you all the time."

"That's right." He patted his right-hand pocket and pulled out an old-fashioned key ring, attached by a gold chain to his pants belt loop.

"You'd have been better off with another combination lock, Mr. Martel. This is Boy Scout stuff."

When a key goes in a lock, time after time after time, it starts to wear the tumblers down. They become smooth, slightly worn. I took a penlight out of my sport coat jacket. "Get your magnifying glass. I want to show you something."

"It's in my middle desk drawer," Martel said. "You get the damn thing."

Good old Claude. Cautious to the end. I got the magnifying glass and held it at an angle until the beam of the small flashlight highlighted the inner works of the lock on box number seven.

I took a quick peek, then called Martel over. "Take a look. You'll see some small scratch marks."

He put on his glasses and peered at the magnifying glass. "This is all supposed to signify something important, I suppose."

"Yes, tell us what we're supposed to see, Mr. Polo."

I spun around to find Lionel Martel standing at the opening to the vault. His left arm was still in a sling. He paused at the entrance. "May I come in, Father?"

"Yes, yes." Claude Martel fumed. "Now just what is going on, Polo?"

"Why don't you tell him, Lionel?" I said.

"Me? I'm as confused as Father. Do go on."

"You know what had me fooled at first, Lionel? The fingertip. I didn't think you'd have the guts to cut that off."

Claude Martel's voice boomed around the room. "Lionel, what is he talking about? Damn it. I—"

Lionel held out a quieting hand. "I don't know, Father. But let's not wake up the neighborhood. Let's hear what Mr. Polo has to say."

"I was just showing your father how the lock had been picked on box number seven here. Was it just number seven, or did you have a peek at all of the boxes?"

Lionel leaned back against the vault door and smiled sullenly. "I don't have any idea what you're talking about. But go ahead. It's an interesting theory."

"Oh, you planned it very well, I have to give you that, Lionel. You had to, to make your father believe it. The House the Homeless benefit was just what you needed, wasn't it? A big party, lots of suspects. You even made sure there was a newspaper woman, Jane Tobin, there, so that the story would make the press before your father could squash it. Your sister told me a couple of interesting family secrets. One was that your father had no trust in you at all and would never allow you to take over the company, even after his death. The only way to find out for sure if that was the truth would be to check his will, and the Martel, Inc. formation papers." I tapped box number seven. "You'd been in the vault enough times with your father, you knew where he kept the really important documents. It was too much of a temptation for you. You had to find out what was in there. So while he was away in Europe, you played burglar."

"I wouldn't have the slightest idea on how to open those boxes. I've always been afraid to go near them. They're hooked up to a burglar alarm, for God's sake."

"Right. A simple hookup, which any burglar given the time, and the location of the switchbox, could handle with ease. Even a butcher like Patrick Lanagan. You went to

Whitman first, didn't you? He didn't have the expertise to open the boxes, but he knew someone who did, Pat Lanagan. So you had them over. With your father in Europe and Michelle out of the house, they could look the vault over at their leisure. So you got into box number seven and saw the will, didn't you? And it left you out in left field. That's when you got the idea about stealing the paintings. Or did Whitman or Lanagan plant that little seed into your head?"

Claude Martel put his hand to his forehead and sagged down into a chair by the desk. "Lionel, this cannot be true. It—"

"It's not, Father. The man is making it up. Trying to make himself look good after bungling his job."

Michelle Martel walked into the vault, her eyes twisting back and forth, the proverbial kid in a candy shop. "I always wondered just what it looked like in here. I've been listening outside. The conversation is just too fascinating to miss." She turned to her father. "You don't mind, do you, Claude?"

I walked over and sat on the edge of the desk. Any minute now Denise would come in wearing a strapless evening gown and carrying a tray of cocktails.

"Lanagan. That's the other reason I didn't figure you for the job, Lionel. It didn't make sense. If you stole the paintings, you'd have done it at your leisure. One painting at a time. Why was Lanagan at the party? At first I assumed he was the muscle man, the one who'd hit you over the head, tortured you, got you to open the vault, and then hauled the loot out of here. That bothered me, the size of the paintings and all, but it was still a possibility. Once I knew who the red-headed waiter was, that he was Whitman's old partner, it made a little more sense. Still, it was a sore spot. I couldn't figure a reason for Lanagan's being there if you were involved."

Lionel patted his lips and gave a slight yawn. Never should do that. It's like a fighter who takes a heavy punch and then puts on an idiotic smile, as if he enjoyed the punishment.

"Yes, Lionel, you were way at the bottom of my list. Then I remembered something else your loving sister told me."

"What's that?" questioned Michelle.

"That Lionel liked to play doctor with you when you were children."

"God, this is really ridiculous," Lionel said, adjusting the sling around his neck.

"Yes, it is," I agreed. "Nothing at all to do with anything, but it got me thinking. You liked to play doctor with little girls. So maybe you played patient with some big boys. I checked at San Quentin. Patrick Lanagan was working as an aide at the infirmary while a guest of the State of California. Nothing fancy at first. Sweeping out the rooms, bringing the prisoners their food, then graduating to helping the doctors on their appointed rounds, swabbing down arms and asses with alcohol before the needle plunged in. The doctor's recommendation was the reason that Lanagan got out on parole; he said that Lanagan had become really valuable. They get a lot of cuttings and stabbings in San Quentin. A couple of poor souls even got their hands severed and sewed back on. So Lanagan got quite a medical education. Was it Lanagan who came up with the idea of whacking off your fingertip to make the robbery look more realistic? Or was his job just to dispose of the knife and pick up the garbage? The Novocain, needle, and syringes. I spoke to the doctor who treated you at Mt. Zion Hospital, Dr. Chung. He said the cut was clean, 'almost surgical.' He also said that you handled the pain amazingly well. That's because you already had a body full of painkillers, wasn't that it? I don't think Lanagan had cleaned his nails since he left prison, so I hope he wore gloves and you used lots of disinfectant."

"I've had about enough of this," Lionel said, starting to exit the vault.

"No. Stay!" Claude Martel commanded.

Lionel stood with his back to us. He took a deep intake of breath, pushed the vault door shut, then turned around.

"If you insist, Father. But this man is a complete ass. He has no proof at all about this ridiculous story."

He was absolutely right of course, no proof at all. "No proof? Oh, there's proof all right, Lionel," I said in what I hoped was a confident tone. "Plenty of it. Your connection with Whitman to begin with."

"I told you that he did a job for me some time ago. Did it well. That's why I hired him again."

"Yes. The police will get into Whitman's safe, where he kept all his sensitive files, so they'll have all the information about that 'little job.' They'll also find that Whitman was in contact with Chuck Bodine. Is that why you killed Bodine?"

Lionel ran his good hand through his hair. "No, no. You're just making wild accusations. Whitman had done a job for Bodine, too. Chuck was the one who recommended Whitman to me. You're just making things up. Putting together facts that don't fit and trying to make a case out of it."

It was like that point in a football game where a team that has been on the ropes makes a big play, and momentum starts to swing to their side. Big Mo was moving to Lionel's side of the field. Both Claude and Michelle Martel looked at me with doubting eyes.

It was time for the bluff. "It won't work, Lionel. You were seen at the houseboat. Not the day of the explosion. The night before. The night you had Patrick Lanagan show you how he was going to wire the houseboat with the dynamite. How he piled a bunch of cheap paintings on the second bomb so that they'd spray canvas all over the area. The night you killed him. How did you get out of there with the bombs in place? Climb out a window? What happened? Did Whitman and Lanagan want a bigger piece of the ransom? Or did they want the paintings, too? They must have thought they had you over a barrel and could walk away with everything. What was the original plan? To call your father, tell him the paintings were at the houseboat, then blow up the place before anyone got there? Or were you going to let some jerk like me wander over there and break in and blow myself, and the phony paintings, to smithereens?"

Momentum was back on my side now. Little beads of sweat were popping up over Lionel's eyebrows. "But you killed Lanagan first, didn't you? Shot him. The police bomb squad found part of a gun in the wreckage. Then you finished setting up the explosives. You knew Whitman was here at your father's house. When he left here the next morning, it was to meet with you. Then you sent Whitman back to get the money from your father. Once Whitman delivered the satchels with the money, you sent him on his merry way to meet with Lanagan on the houseboat. You had it all now. The cash, the paintings. No problems. Except for Chuck Bodine."

Claude Martel's voice was a croak. "No, Lionel. It's not true. Say it's not true."

"Of course it's not true, Father," Lionel snarled.

"Yes," I said, "Bodine. He worried me. Your father said he was like an uncle to you. But he was more than that, wasn't he? Someone whose shoulder you cried on. Whitman had gotten both of you out from under charges of screwing some teenyboppers. Bodine knew a crook when he saw one, and when he saw Whitman there the night of the supposed robbery, he knew Whitman had to be involved. Then good old Michelle here kept Bodine posted on Whitman, his camping out at the house, the telephone calls. Bodine was no fool. He put two and two together a lot faster than I did. He knew you were involved, didn't he? When someone broke into Bodine's place, he got really upset. Figured it had to be connected with the robbery. He confronted you, didn't he? Told you he was going to tell your father about the robbery if you didn't return the paintings, didn't he? Was he going to go to the police, too? Is that why you ended up killing him?"

"This is preposterous," Lionel protested, reaching in his

pants pocket for a handkerchief and wiping his brow. "I've had enough. Father—"

All eyes turned to Claude Martel. He was holding a big automatic pistol in his hand. "Where are my paintings and my money, Lionel?

"Father, I tell you—"

"Nonsense! You were always a terrible liar! What did you do with my paintings and my money!"

"Father, I—"

Michelle Martel ran over and slapped Lionel across the face.

Lionel raised his arm to hit her back, then wiped his sleeve across his mouth. "Don't get so excited, Michelle," he said with a trace of contempt in his voice. "You were dying to know what was in his will. Well, we're both out of it. When Father dies, everything is sold. All the properties, the galleries, everything. We each get two hundred and fifty thousand: you, me, even Denise. The rest goes to the De Young Museum. All the paintings, all the money, everything, to help build a new museum wing. The Claude Martel wing."

The sound of the gun's going off in the enclosed room was almost as loud as the explosion at the boathouse. The bullet ricocheted off the steel vault door and passed close to my head.

I ducked, then reached out for Claude Martel. He waved the gun at me.

"Don't move. Any of you." He swiveled the barrel back in the direction of his son. "Where are they, Lionel? Where are my paintings and my money?"

"The money is safe. I was going to return it—"

"Where?" Claude roared.

"In my bank, downtown. In my safety-deposit box."

"And the paintings?"

"They're there, too."

Claude Martel heaved a sigh of relief. "Good. Then all is not lost. We will pick them up first thing in the morning."

Lionel was visibly shaking as he stared at his father. "But what about—"

"We'll discuss your future after I get the money and the paintings back."

"You're forgetting a couple of things, Mr. Martel," I said.

He edged the gun barrel over in my direction and said, "Such as?"

"Such as three dead people: Whitman, Lanagan, and your ex-partner, Charles Bodine."

"Mr. Polo, I understand you fancy yourself quite the cardplayer. If you ever got into a game with me, you would leave the table with nothing but the clothes on your back. I know a bluff when I hear one. You frightened Lionel, but you don't frighten me. You have nothing, or you would have given it to the police, rather than coming here and putting on this dramatic charade."

"You don't think enough of your son to trust him with your business. How do you think he handled the killing of three men? Even an explosion doesn't blow away everything. Once the police focus on Lionel, they'll come up with a connection. His fingerprints on some of the debris from the houseboat. Someone's seeing him with Whitman, and Lanagan. A man with a sling is someone people remember." I edged closer to Martel as I spoke. The gun in his hand looked like a .45 automatic. He kept his eyes on me and gently slapped the gun's barrel into the palm of his left hand. You could almost hear the wheels going around in his head.

I turned to Lionel. "Killing Bodine was a mistake. Especially doing such a hasty job. Where'd you do it, Lionel? My guess is your building's garage. Somehow you got Bodine down there alone. By the trunk of his car. Maybe you'd even turned over the paintings to him. When he put them in the trunk, you knifed him in the back, then dumped him in the trunk and slit his throat. The police will check around. There may be some blood on the garage floor. Or the garage attendant will remember the Jaguar. Maybe even remember you in it. And your trip back from the airport. They'll start checking—"

"Shut up," Claude Martel said, his voice low and razor sharp now. Gone was the confusion, hate, and fear. He just sat there tapping the gun in his palm, looking at me. He was one cold-blooded bastard.

"He's right, Son." Martel stood up and repeated himself. "He's right, Son." He pointed the .45 at Lionel and said, "Look at him, Mr. Polo. Just look."

I twisted my head toward Lionel Martel. It may have been my imagination, but I thought I felt a rush of air hit the back of my head before the gun butt did. I was halfway to the carpet when the second blow put me into dreamland.

32

I woke up on the carpeted floor of the vault. I reached and groped around the back of my head with one hand. It came back smeared with blood. I started the arduous journey up to my knees, then finally to my feet. But not for long. I fell back to the floor. Remembering a wise man's words, 'If at first you don't succeed, maybe you're doing something wrong, stupid,' I got to my hands and knees and crawled over to a chair, then pulled myself up inch by inch. I finally got seated and went back to probing around the back of my head. There seemed to be two separate wounds, both covered with matted blood. I sat, bent over, taking deep, slow breaths. What scared me most was that my vision was blurred. I kept blinking, but it didn't seem to change anything.

I looked around the vault. It was like watching a TV set slightly out of focus. Claustrophobia had never been a problem before. Of course I'd never been locked in a vault before. I told myself that Martel had spent hours in there. There had to be a good ventilation system. No problem. Unless someone decided to turn it off. The room seemed to shrink when that little gem popped into my dented head.

I found that by squinting, my vision seemed to improve

a bit. So I squinted around the room, looking for the telephones on the desk. They were no longer there. I was breathing fast and deep, like a swimmer getting ready to go to the bottom of the pool. I gave myself a little pep talk; calm down, breathe slowly, there's all kinds of air, calm down. Easy for you to say, I told myself. It was that kind of a pep talk.

I'm not sure how long I sat there talking to myself, but gradually my breathing did slow down to something close to normal. I peered around the vault again. No sense trying the door. Claude Martel had demonstrated the fact that you needed the combination to get out, as well as get in. Which left what? I tilted my head back painfully and looked at the ceiling. Fluorescent lights. No help. Smoke alarm. As Mrs. Damonte loved to say, "Bingo!"

Or was it. It could be hooked up to an outside alarm company, which would bring the alarm company and the fire department. Or it could just be in-house, which would bring back nothing but Claude Martel and his big gun. Either way, it was an improvement over sitting there and scaring myself to death.

I knew I didn't have any matches on me, but I stupidly patted my pockets anyway. Not only no matches, but nothing else either. The Martels had cleaned out my pockets. Then I tried the desk. Martel must have some firepower to stroke those cigars of his. No matches. No lighter. One of his cigar butts was crushed out in the desk ashtray. I touched the end. Dead cold.

I could break up the chair I was sitting in and rub the wooden legs together until fire appeared. Given the amount of energy pouring through my rapidly aging body, that would only take a week or two. Besides, have you ever heard of that actually working? It's one of the reasons for the high desertion rate in the Boy Scouts. That and the fact that girls laugh at them in their uniforms.

Martel had taken my watch along with everything else,

so I got back on the floor and lay there waiting. I don't know if it was twenty minutes or a couple of hours later when the vault door started to open. I was on my knees again by the time it was opened far enough for Denise Martel to come in carrying a tray. My earlier vision had been a premonition. No strapless gown, just powder-blue pants and a matching turtleneck. Claude was right behind her, the automatic in his hand.

Denise knelt beside me and made sympathetic clucking sounds as she got me to my feet and back in the chair.

"Poor man, are you all right?" she asked, her fingers feeling around the back of my head.

I brushed her hand away. "Just dandy, thanks."

"Sorry about that, Polo," Claude Martel said. "I'll let you out of here in the morning. You'll be well paid for your troubles."

"What's the going rate of pay for having your head bashed in, Martel?"

"We'll settle it in the morning."

"After you get your money and paintings back from Lionel?"

"Yes, after that. And after Lionel has left the country."

Poor Lionel. After killing three men and stealing millions of dollars, Daddy was probably going to banish him to a mansion in Brazil. I hoped the least he got was a bad sunburn, or herpes from the girl from Ipanema. I didn't know just how much of the scenario I had made up about Lionel's involvement in the robbery and murders was true, but there was certainly enough truth in it to send him scurrying away, after handing over the money and paintings to dear old Dad, of course.

The tray Denise Martel settled on top of the desk had a glass, a pitcher of water, an ice bucket, a bottle of Jack Daniel's, and what looked like some kind of sandwich.

She noticed my interest. "What can I fix you, Nick?"

"Nothing, thanks." I grabbed some ice and popped it in

my mouth while Denise put some cubes in a linen napkin and applied it to the back of my neck.

"That's enough, Denise. Let's leave Mr. Polo to himself until the morning."

"It won't work, Martel. It's just a matter of time before the cops connect Lionel to all of what's happened."

He shrugged indifferently. "Lionel will be where the police won't find him. Whatever evidence the police do turn up will be inconclusive, or at least open to conjecture by the attorneys I'll hire."

Denise just stood there pouting, the ever-loyal wife. Wonderful family. I wondered what they gave old Claude on Father's Day. More pins for his voodoo dolls?

Either there was something in the ice, or the effects of the whacks on the back of my head were coming back. The room got blurry again and started spinning.

Someone came in the vault. It looked like Michelle Martel. She said, "There's a man to see you, Father." No, I thought just before the lights went out again. She'd never call him Father.

33

I knew it couldn't be heaven. There was too much of a smell of antiseptics in the air. Unless Mrs. Damonte had preceded me and had started cleaning the place up. The face looking down at me was serious. It was also directly under a starched white cap.

"Kowalski? Is that you?" I said, the words seeming to stick on my lips before they got out where someone could hear them.

"Relax, Mr. Polo. My name is Jorgenson. The doctor just left. You're going to be fine. There are some visitors waiting to see you. Are you up to it?"

"Sure. But first tell me, where am I?"

"San Francisco General Hospital. You've got a concussion. You'll be fine, but you'll be in the hospital for a few days." She backed away from the bed as she spoke. Even with my fuzzy vision I could see she didn't look anything like nurse Kowalski. The two people who came in the room looked just like Inspector Robert Tehaney and Jane Tobin. And they were. Two out of three wasn't bad in my condition.

Jane got to me first.

"Nick, are you all right?"

"According to nurse Jorgenson, I'll survive. Are you here as a loving friend, or newspaper woman?"

"Get wise, Nicky, and I'll let you eat the hospital food rather than the goodies Mrs. Damonte has waiting for you."

Tehaney bent over the bed, gave me a good look, then said, "I'll be back tomorrow."

"Wait, Bob. Don't go yet. What happened? I remember passing out in the vault. Nothing after that until a few minutes ago."

"My office got an anonymous tip. Said I should get over to the Martel house right away. Michelle Martel met me at the door and led me to that fancy vault." He reached for his cigarettes, saw the NO SMOKING sign, and put them back in his pocket.

"Anyway, you passed out for a while, came to, mumbling something about Lionel Martel's killing Bodine, Whitman, and Lanagan, passed right out again, then all hell broke loose. The Martels were screaming and shouting like you wouldn't believe. Half of it in French, but I got the drift."

"Did you arrest Lionel Martel?"

"No." He went back to his cigarette pack and lit up, peeking over his shoulder like a schoolyard kid afraid of the teacher catching him. "Not yet. But we're working on it."

"The money and the paintings. They're supposed to be in Lionel Martel's bank."

"I know. I know. The Martel daughter dumped on that." He looked at his wrist. "I'm going down to his bank now. It should be quite a show. Talk to you later."

I couldn't make out the hands on the wall clock and asked Jane the time.

"A little after nine."

"In the morning?"

"Yes. I guess you did take a pretty good rap on your head, Nick."

I reached up to touch my head and found it was bandaged, from front to back.

"You look something like a half-done mummy," Jane said.

My eyelids felt as if they were being forced down. I dropped off to sleep, and when I woke up, Jane was gone. I dozed on and off, being interrupted by occasional visits from doctors and nurses, who would shine lights in my eyes, take my pulse, stick needles in my arm, and smile noncommittally when I asked how I was doing.

It went on like that for some time. Once I woke up and found Jane and Mrs. Damonte herself sitting alongside the bed. I mumbled a few words and went right back to dreamland. Then I woke up again and everything looked wonderful. No headache. No fuzzy double vision. I could see the clock perfectly. I could even see the subtle pattern in my visitor's tie.

"How are you feeling?" Gene Lembi asked.

"Not bad. Not bad at all. What day is it?"

"Friday."

It was on Wednesday that I had been sapped in Martel's vault. "Tell me what's going on. Did you get your painting back?"

Lembi grunted. "Painting. Claude Martel claims it is not an original van Gogh. Claims it's a copy, and he has some high-powered appraiser willing to testify to that fact."

"Is it a fake?"

"No. It's the original. There's no doubt in my mind. The other painting was a Renoir. Martel claims that is a fake also." Lembi sighed and leaned against the bed rail. "But it will be a long battle, my friend. I will have the van Gogh appraised also. It will end up going to court. Art experts are like psychiatrists when they testify in court. They tend to go in the direction they're being paid." His gaze seemed to turn inward, like a blind man's. "In the meantime, Claude Martel has possession of the paintings. The local police claim they have no reason to take charge of them. Martel never did report them missing. He's very clever. I'm afraid he'll find a way to dispose of them before a judge can make a ruling. Whatever, it will take years. I've hired an attorney, but unfortunately, Martel can probably wait me out." He held out his hand. "I'm going back to France, but I'll keep in touch."

Lembi had no sooner limped out of the room when Bob Tehaney came in. He and Lembi exchanged words in the corridor for a minute, then Tehaney dragged a chair over to my bed.

"Can you talk now, hotshot?" he asked.

I did. Into Tehaney's tape recorder. When he was finished with his questions and had turned the machine off, I asked him, "How's the case going, Bob?"

"Like shit. I know Lionel Martel's our boy, but it's going to be tough. I can tie him in with Whitman. Several people saw them together before the explosion. I guess that's when Whitman passed him his father's money. But I haven't got him at the houseboat yet."

"What about the Bodine murder?"

"Looks better on that. Lionel really wet his pants when I first questioned him. But his old man has pulled out all the stops. Hired three of the best lawyers in the country to defend the kid. Three of the bastards. Can you imagine that?"

"No luck on finding out where Bodine was actually killed?"

"Nope. Not yet."

I told Tehaney my theory about Lionel Martel's stabbing Chuck Bodine while he was putting something in the trunk of the Jaguar.

"Yeah. We thought of that. We're checking out the garage in the building where Lionel lives, but nothing so far. There is one thing left to do, though, Nicky?"

"What's that?"

"You. You want to charge Martel with assault? Sign a complaint? He put a couple of pretty heavy creases in that hard head of yours. Doctor told me you were hit three times. One more good pop might have been enough to kill you."

"I really hadn't thought about that, Bob. Sure. Why

not? Martel will just put some of his high-power legal eagles on it, but it'll cost him some time and money. Yeah, I'll sign a complaint."

Tehaney's lips spread in a toothy smile. "He'll either hire the attorneys or try and buy you off, Nick. I'll have someone from the DA's office stop by with the complaint."

When the doctor came in a little later, he seemed as happy as I was about my progress and said that if things continued to look good, I'd be released in the morning.

I was telling Jane Tobin the good news. She had come armed with some more of Mrs. Damonte's goodies: artichoke frittata and pine-nut breadsticks.

Michelle Martel came in just as we were finishing lunch. After I made the introductions, Jane got up and said she was going out for a little fresh air.

Michelle was all dressed up in motorcycle chic: black leather pants, a black T-shirt with a Harley emblem on it. Her belt was a chrome-plated motorcycle chain, her jacket, black leather, with long, cowboy-style fringe hanging from the sleeves. Her sunglasses were a dark black plastic, the frame the same shade as the lenses. She was a good ten years too old for the outfit, but I certainly wasn't going to tell her so. Not with the violent streak that ran in the Martel family.

"I guess I should thank you for that anonymous call to the cops, Michelle."

She took off her glasses and gave the room a quick once-over. "Not exactly the Top of the Mark, is it, Polo?"

"It's amazing how little you care for the decor when you're worried about your bashed-in head." I patted the mattress. "Sit down."

She chose a chair alongside the bed.

"How did your father take it? He must know you're the one who called the police."

"He wasn't very happy. But then he never is." She twirled the sunglasses in her hand. "I think he's feeling a

211

little guilty about what happened. I'm sure he'd be willing to have you moved to a more comfortable hospital."

"I'm happy here. Should be out in the morning. But why all this concern about my comforts?"

She shrugged. "He feels sorry, that's all."

"What's he feel about you? I thought by now you'd be kicked out of the house and banned from the galleries."

"He thought about it, I'm sure. But if there's one thing Claude is, it's practical. He doesn't want me talking to the police."

"And the price for your silence?"

The glasses were twirling faster now. "We have an understanding. There're going to be some changes." She dropped the glasses in her lap and leaned forward. "Claude never had much love or respect for me, Polo. I learned to live with that. Now he does have a feeling about me. Fear." She fell back in the chair. "Intoxicating feeling, having someone fear you. There are going to be some changes. Even in his will. My attorney is talking to his attorney. There'll be guarantees."

Attorneys. Divorce, rape, murder, incest, earthquakes, plane crashes—no matter what the catastrophe, they're there to help. And skim off the cream. No wonder Mom tried pushing me toward law school.

"I followed you the other day. From Islais Creek. You were pulling up the rear for Chuck Bodine. I didn't know you two were that friendly."

"Chuck and I had an understanding. I helped him, and when the time was right, he was going to help me."

"You mean you dumped everything you could find out about Martel, Inc., then when Bodine took over, he'd offer you a job."

"Something like that. But Chuck's gone now."

That certainly was one way of putting it. "So you and Daddy and Brother are all one big happy family again, Michelle?"

"Something like that," she repeated. "We would appreciate your cooperation. You'd be paid handsomely."

Handsomely. That had a nice ring to it. "And I bet I wouldn't have to work very hard to earn this money, huh? Just lose my memory? A bang on the head can cause amnesia, I'm told."

She smiled knowingly, stood up, reached into her jacket, and came out with a white envelope. It looked well stuffed.

"I told Claude we could count on you," she said, pushing the envelope in my direction.

I took it, hefted it in my hand, feeling the weight. Even if it was stuffed with five- or ten-dollar bills, it was a nice package. I tore open the envelope. No fives or tens. All nice, crisp one-hundred-dollar bills. Claude Martel seemed to have a surplus of them. I took out eight of the bills, then tossed the envelope back to her. "That's the eight hundred dollars Lionel owed me from the poker game. Tell your father I'm signing a complaint against him this afternoon. For assault, battery, and anything else the district attorney can think of."

"You're being stupid. Claude can crush you."

"No. He can crush you or Lionel or Denise. But not me. I'm cooperating with the police. They're going to make life miserable for the Martels. And your half brother is going to go to jail on a homicide charge. I don't care how much Daddy spends in legal fees, Tehaney will nail Lionel."

Her eyes narrowed. There was a gleam in them. Then she slipped on her sunglasses. "So long, sucker," she said.

I watched her leather-covered fanny swish out the door. She was tougher than her miserable father. No wonder that gleam in the eye. She'd love to see Lionel get convicted. That would give her the whip hand. Once Lionel was behind bars, Claude Martel had better watch his back. And have his butler start up his car in the morning. I had the feeling Tehaney was going to get some more anonymous tips if

Michelle felt the case against her brother wasn't proceeding along the right lines.

Jane came trotting back and sat down on the bed.

"What did the lonesome cowgirl want?" she asked.

"Michelle Martel. Wanted to make sure I was comfortable."

"And are you?"

I scratched my head where the bandages met the flesh of my neck. "No, not really. I can't wait to get out of here."

"Well, the doctor did say tomorrow's the day. You can stay at my place until you're a hundred percent."

She saw the concerned look on my face and gently ran her hand up and down my leg. "Don't worry, Mrs. Damonte will continue to supply the food. I'll take care of the rest."

Ah, the best of both worlds, I thought as I settled back against the pillows. Every once in a while we all deserve it.